PARADISE RODRIGUEZ

Finding Paradise

Devereux
PUBLISHING

First published by Devereux Publishing 2019

Paradise Rodriguez is the sole founder of The Catch A Falling Star Foundation. Should you find yourself in immediate danger, always call 911 first.

Front cover photographer: Ranjit Patel

Back cover photographer: Reggie Garrett

First edition

ISBN: 978-0-578-55109-8

Proofreading by Mark Drum

"You can sit in the corner and cry or you can go out and dance in the rain. Either way, the storm is coming."

-PARADISE RODRIGUEZ 2008

Contents

1

I have an idea...

There comes a pivotal moment in everyone's life where you are utterly exhausted. You've grown tired of trying to be everything for everyone and trying to always explain yourself when you aren't even exactly sure who you are. You feel the darkness surrounding you. You try to find a shriveled glimpse of light, but it's too late. You are consumed in your personal black hole, desiring to know..."what next?" It's not always a direct sadness you feel, but a sense of being lost. You know what you want, and you see it, but you haven't the slightest clue as to how to retrieve it. Daily, you search for ways to bridge the gap between where you are and where you want to be. You dig and mold, trying to build something out of nothing until one day, you decide to leave it all behind. Well, I am currently sitting on the floor drinking wine out of the bottle (the epitome of class, right?) staring at the two suitcases that I am supposed to pack a month, quite possibly, my entire life into....while keeping their weights under 10kg and 20Kg. F...M...L (For those who don't speak text, FUCK MY LIFE).

These airlines are crazy. Hell, I am crazy. I can't believe I am seriously about to do this! What led me to this impromptu decision could seemingly be summed up into one phrase. Circumstances had become, by the very definition, life or death - and I am choosing life. You see, growing up, I had a rather pathetic "childhood." You know the story, it's been told a dozen times. A child is born, the father takes off, the mother abuses the child throughout their childhood (unless of course, she was gaining something beneficial from the child), the mother later births several other children that the first has to raise. Sad, right?! Well, it gets even more morbid.

You see, I have five profound W.T.F. (What The Fuck), wall-building moments that put me on this path. My name is Anaís, and this is my story.

Moment 1: He didn't come.

My father told me at six years old, "I'll see you tomorrow. 11 am sharp." then he left. Fast forward to 10 am the next morning. I was sitting on the front stairs waiting for my father, where I sat waiting until midnight that night. He never came. Little did he know, I had up-cycled (fashion term for recycling) one of my dresses, and I was very excited to show him. Why wasn't he there? I had behaved so well. Even did extra chores. Why did he not come for me? Was I not good enough? What could have been so important that he didn't pick up and get his daughter like he promised? These would be the questions that would haunt me for several years. It was then that the walls were first formed. From there I went through a series of "bad boyfriends" from the age of 15 until…well, maybe I'm still kind of going through that. There was this one guy…but we will come back to "*HIM*…"

Moment 2: She's gone...forever

As if mother's abusive boyfriends, us being evicted (moving every two months) and me going through a serious "mask" phase wasn't enough...I woke up on the morning of December 30th, 2007, only to find my baby sister DEAD. Yes, you read that correctly. I was born rather ill, being what we call a "super-preemie". I was born at 22 weeks with all sorts of health issues that resulted in me having to wear one of those creepy face masks everywhere. Needless to say, I was a "freak" in the eyes of the other kids, and that left me without having any friends. I had another sibling at the time that was a boy, but I desperately wanted a little sister. They say God tends to give us what we seek so be careful with what we ask for. I used to say, "Why do I have to be the only one who is always sick?" A few years later, around the age of 8, mother randomly packs us up in her baby blue Dodge Neon and takes us to Louisiana. There she confessed, after a series of odd questions like, "If a baby was sick, like really sick, would you want it to be in our family?", that she was pregnant with what turned out to be my awesome baby sister and that she was going to be born with a lot of significant health complications. Hell if I cared, I was finally getting a little sister! Seven years I got with my princess...well, seven years she was alive. I spent some of that time bouncing between two abusive homes. One of my biggest regrets was not staying with her full time, but life happens, right? My walls super-sized after I found her dead; her little body was just too tired to go on. My life forever changed that day.

Moment 3: Meet "dumb" Anaís.

Growing up in Chicago was the equivalent of walking through all nine circles of Hell without ever actually making it through. Much to many surprise, I'm actually quite intelligent. I always have been. I just didn't like to show it. I used to, though. I loved being smart, but to others it wasn't "acceptable." Mother used to say, "No one likes a smart ass." and then when I would get just one thing wrong, she'd be quick to tell me how stupid I was. I was never good enough for her. The kids at school were just as bad. They made fun of my accent since I spoke French. English was not my mother tongue.

I was told that I wasn't "black enough" due to my high yellow skin color and that white people didn't belong in their school. I never knew what that meant per se, but I understood what they were implying. They liked to cut chunks out of my hair, and Heaven forbid I aced an exam! I'd get trapped in the classroom, and my face punched for being a "show off nerd". Long story short, I did not fit in at all. Thus, the start of my "dumbing down phase". I thought I wanted to be like them. I thought if I just sounded "black" and acted like the class idiot, maybe people would stop harassing me. I wasn't the only one. The darker black kids that were the brains, were treated very similarly. Unfortunately, I was the only one in class with such a mixed heritage, and being so fair-skinned made me the ultimate target.

I'm French, Irish, and Puerto Rican/Spaniard. I learned that my maternal Gran was from Ireland, and grand-père (biological grandfather) was from France. My paternal Abuelita was Native, but had been born and raised in Puerto Rico and Avi (R.I.P.), my paternal grandfather, was from Spain. I didn't find out why I looked so different until I was in my 10th year, but by then it was too late. I had already tried so hard to fit in and ruined my life. I thought if I JUST… but the joke was on me because I then fell into a horrible habit. I tried so hard to brown my skin then grades dramatically dropped until I ran away to Santa Monica. Things were better in Santa Monica...until mother brought her another abusive boyfriend to my home. The beatings triggered me, and back to "dumb" Anaís, I went. This time, I didn't fall out of the phase. It lasted until I lost myself completely.

Moment 4: HIM

I met a boy. I had no clue what I was getting myself into, but it happened faster than a strike of lightening. I met a boy, I loved the boy, and my heart was shattered by the boy. Of course, things weren't that simple - and still aren't. It wasn't all his fault; we both had poor judges of character in our lives that were always interjecting their inferior opinions into our relationship. Add the issue that we didn't have decent examples of a functioning relationship to look up to with us merely not being mature enough...and it was a recipe for disaster. There was also the fact that he was my mirror. As destructive as I was...so was he. We were so alike, yet so different. He was a coward in many ways, and I was overly confrontational in most, but when it was just us, I could almost swear that the earth stood still. Have you ever met a person, and you just knew they were going to significantly impact your life? That was us.

It was a Thursday evening, and I'd entered what had quickly become my preferred lounge. I saw him in the middle of an exchange with a girl I'd previously met two weeks prior. Deciding the situation would require a bit of tact, I chose to walk past them both only displaying a smile. I observed the situation, mentally plotting my next move. He was preoccupied with a discourse with his friend and an unfamiliar

5

bloke. He was average height, standing approximately at 5'10", with long, shaggy hair that he pulled into a bun. I could tell he worked out. He was built with such defined arms. I allowed myself to imagine, for a moment, what it might be like to have those arms wrapped around me. Relishing in the thought, I decided it was time to make my presence known. I stepped towards him like a lioness moving in on her prey. The friend introduced me to him, and at once, everything seemed to fall silent. It was as if the entire world disappeared, leaving just the two of us. It wasn't the color of his eyes that captivated me, but what laid beneath them. The blue hues carried such currents that made it impossible to escape, and before I could catch my breath, I was drowning in them. His eyes were deceptively limped, changing from an icy blue to having muted tones of green. He didn't know, but I had a *thing* with eyes. I have always believed them to be the gateways to the soul, and so it is the first thing I notice about a person. He looked at me with such guileless eyes, but his lips spoke with ardent tones. It was intoxicating. He smelled of danger, but I wasn't afraid. I said to him, "You're an asshole, but I'm going to be your best friend." He expressed a devilish grin and simply said, "Okay." Our eyes locked for what seemed like an eternity. He had me, but I wasn't going to let him know that...not yet.

A year later, things heated up quickly between us. He told me he loved me before either of us had officially made a move. Three months later, he asked me to be his girlfriend, and three months after that, his wife. We fell fast, but damn, we fell hard. We had an incredible relationship filled with immeasurable passion and desire, yet also filled with great pain and chaos. Kisses turned into punches. "I love you," turned into, "I want to hate you." It was more than complicated. But even on the worst days, like sitting in the hospital with a failing heart alone, I still loved him…a part of me always will I think…even if I don't remember it all.

Which moves us to (drum roll please)…Moment 5: Paradise lost.

Things in my life were so disastrous that my brain broke. No, I'm serious…my brain literally broke. After a series of "I hate you" – "I love you," among other things, it turned out to be a rather hellacious winter, spring, and summer. So, in the fall of 2014, I finally broke. One, not so pleasant night, I was feeling quite overwhelmed after yet another fight with H.I.M. I stupidly went for a drive to clear my head. I had decided I was leaving town, but I needed to vent to the universe and clear my mind. I called on a friend, and we drove to the beach. I guess it was rather senseless to allow the girl who is ranting and crying to drive, but when I want to do something, no one can truly stop me. So, she didn't, and I ran her car into a light post. The damages weren't too terrible for her car, but I did hit my head. Much to my surprise, me hitting my head didn't do this. Me allowing everyone to walk on me, me constantly trying to live up to other people's standards, me always trying to be there for everyone else, and me choosing to not practice self-care…yes that is what did this to me. I destroyed myself by neglecting myself all those years, and it finally caught up with me. I'd awaken the next day feeling extremely disorientated, not really knowing who or where I was. After a series of panic attacks and exams, it was concluded that I was suffering from an unfortunate combination of Anterograde and Retrograde Amnesia, the result from having long term unchecked complex PTSD. I had lost about 5 years of memories (including all memories of H.I.M. and me). I was fucked.

The first 8 months were incredibly difficult. I spent most of them just getting used to my career while trying to understand and relearn the memories I lost. There were times it would be as if my mind was frozen in place, attempting to recall a moment in time. Then, there were the nights I'd have dreams and nightmares as vivid as memories. The trouble was, there were only two ways to confirm these memory flashes and that was to re-read my old journals and asking *HIM*, which only left me further confused. I decided to avoided human interaction as much as possible except for one person, the devil himself, Derek. Why is he the devil? Well, I hope you're sitting down because this psychologically handicapped me for 3 months straight. Derek had been pretending to be like a big brother to me for the last two and a half years. We did pretty much everything together. If I ever needed boy advice, I'd go directly to him, and he'd attempt to guide me and protect me. Anytime he destroyed his life (which was quite often) by not paying his bills or allowing his health to falter, there I was ready to fix it. He taught me patience, and I taught him confidence. We were an impenetrable team! I hadn't realized I had been enabling him, and making the danger I was in, direr.

While in Miami, it was revealed that my mother tried to have an abortion. I survived it, and that is why I was born so sick. I called Derek upset about it, and I also called Him. Derek had been jealous of Him, but I often made excuses for his behavior, convincing myself that he was just being a big brother and just trying to protect me. The truth is, Derek often acted an ass anytime I brought a guy around that I really liked. Maybe if I listened to my gut back then, it would have protected me from what happened next.

Derek became increasingly possessive, so I told him he could not go with me on an upcoming work trip. Everything changed. While I was at my summit, he failed to pay the bills, even though I put money inside of our money box and all he needed to do was call the companies and make the deposits. Derek wasn't very good at keeping up responsibilities, but that didn't stop him from creeping on me. One night, I walked out of my shower only to find him in my bedroom, the same bedroom that was connected to my bathroom. When I asked him what was he doing in there, he made up some excuse and left the house for three days. The situation only got worse from there. Derek had been caught attempting to break into my bedroom on several occasions by our housemates. He eventually stole very special photos - then hid them from me. I pose for art galleries sometimes, but because of the context of the images, I had the only copies...and he took those. When confronted about it all, his response was simply, "So what?" This creep, who had been pretending to be my family, watched me fall into a daily panic about the stalker who had followed us from our apartment to the house, sending unnerving letters to me. I became more frightened after my car was vandalized while I was at a summit in Las Vegas. Derek watched as I suffered through that pain. It turned out to be him that was causing this the entire time. The chaos didn't stop there. The home we were living in, the house I was helping him pay the mortgage on, he signed away then lied about it for months! I found out after a friend caught him in one of his acts. He's a sociopath, and I was a fool to ever trust him. I had given everything to another person. All of my time, energy, effort, and money...gone, wasted. I felt completely defeated.

I sat there wondering how the hell my life turned out like this.

Why do I trust the wrong people? What do I want? I realized that I was depressed and that I was feeling very uninspired. How am I supposed to build my empire while swimming in a sea of darkness?

After a tremendous and emotional collapse, I decided, FUCK IT...FUCK THEM...FUCK IT ALL! Why keep stressing about people and things that don't bring me any joy. I am a good person. I do more for charities than I do for myself. I am always available for everyone all of the time. Maybe that is what the issue is, I am always there...but who is going to be there for me? Am I even there for me? The truthful answer was no one, and no. That needed to change and change quickly. So, I let go of anything I didn't really need, and I took every penny I had to my name, found a flight reservation, and I began planning it all out. My 2017 European Adventure. I was starting in N.Y.C. then going on to Paris – London – Dublin – Milan – Florence – Rome – Barcelona – then back to Paris. I wasn't sure how this worked or how long I'd be gone. I knew I had enough money for a month, and so that is what I was starting with. May 9th- June 9th, a month-long adventure that I am calling... #FindingParadise.

I know, I know! It's absolutely ludicrous and quite possibly mental! Who just drops everything and disappears to Europe? Well, I'm not exactly sure how many people have done it, but I know it is definitely my time. I feel like I need to do this. I don't really know what I am doing, this will be my very first time traveling across Europe like this. I also haven't actually done that much research and planning of this trip, but perhaps that's exactly what I need. Adventure. Since, for so long, my life had been completely out of my control, I spent my adult years trying to control every single aspect of my life. Fact is, we are not in control of everything thing that happens to us, and there is not a damn thing I can do about it. So why not go on an epic adventure...at the very least I will gain some perspective out of it all...and perhaps try some fantastic food too. There was also the case of finding my distant relatives. My happy place was lost, and I needed to find where I belonged.

So here I am, sitting on the floor, drinking wine out of the bottle, staring at two suitcases. Time to stop thinking about it all and get to packing - I leave tomorrow.

After all, Paris is ALWAYS a good idea.

2

Is this really happening?

7:48 am - I could hardly sleep last night. I was so restless about this trip. I drank a whole bottle of wine and was still wide-awake. Eventually, I crashed about a quarter to 6 in the morning…only to wake up at 7:30 am.

Feeling slightly anxious, I ended up RE-packing…again. I was so worried about luggage weight. My bullshit meter kept ringing…I just didn't know what about yet. I was hoping things would go well getting to NYC. It was a 66-hour Greyhound ride to NYC and Greyhound can be the worst! I actually think it's just that people that are awful with terrible communication skills. I don't understand coming to work and not wanting to work. It's like, if you hate your job so much, QUIT! I was sure there were other people who would work that job with honor and respect. Oh well, I'll get there safely, at least…I hope.

As I was boarding the bus, there weren't many seats open. I was beginning to feel frustrated when a woman beckoned me to sit next to her. Feeling grateful, I took the seat. I quickly realized that the woman was more than a bit overweight and was taking some of my seat too. She couldn't help it, in fact, she tried hard to squeeze all her fat into her tiny chair. I felt so badly for her. I told her she was okay, not to worry. I couldn't imagine being a bigger person and trying to stuff yourself into a tiny spot as not to bother another person. I'm somewhat surprised they didn't make her purchase two seats. I hear on airplanes they do. That must be so embarrassing.

On the one hand, I think, "just lose the weight," but on the other hand, she probably tried. It's probably very hard. She often looked over and smiled at me. I soon after realized that she, nor her friends, spoke English and I don't speak fluent Spanish. It was interesting and yet lovely that we were still able to communicate. We all looked out for each other too. At one of the rest stops, the driver was trying to pull off, but I told him they were not back yet and to wait and when I could not find the next station bay, one of the ladies grabbed me and took me to it. My faith in humanity was slowly returning.

One of the stops tonight was Charlotte, NC. Outside the Greyhound station were these old railroad tracks. I decided to take photos of them because they reminded me a bit of me. Once upon a time, travelers used those tracks, but now…now that they're falling apart, someone has just left them to be just broken and *just* there. Were they ever appreciated? I wanted more than that for me. I *am* going to have more than that for me!

22 more hours to go…

3

Sleep is overrated

After an exhausting drive to NYC, I finally made it to JFK airport. Currently sitting at my boarding gate and waiting to board, I looked out the window trying to relax. It was a full moon tonight. The moon, an orb of soft light emitting from the darkness above, such a soothing sight for sore eyes. Blushingly radiant, lighting up a dark night with the hope that radiates through the dark hours of one's life. I find solace in the moon's glow and how fitting that it should be a full moon at the start of something that would be so transitional for me.

The food was overpriced, and some of the people were LOUD. Airports, or really, any public place are kind of like that, but it's okay…as long as it's quiet on the plane. I'm going to need rest; I haven't slept since I woke up on the bus still, at seven this morning. When the bus turned into the station about nine this morning, I didn't really have anywhere to go once we got to NYC. The few people I knew that lived there were either sleeping or M.I.A. I ended up deciding to just go to JFK to wait for my flight…for 13 freaking hours.

Getting out of the Greyhound and to JFK was a little unusual.

I spent a great deal of time running in circles, but I met a random stranger named Larry. He walked me back and forth to find a Bank of America ATM and figure out how to get on the shuttle from the Greyhound station to JFK. He gave me some travel advice, telling me to keep hold of all of my things and to be careful while I'm out there, then set off to complete his day, I assume. He was kind, and I wanted to get a photo, but I didn't want to be rude, so I left it alone.

As I was riding the shuttle to JFK, we started passing things that I had not seen whenever I visit NYC. I only work my events and then leave. I really needed to spend more time there. When we passed Berkeley, the tears started pouring down my face. Berkeley was on my list of colleges that I wanted to attend. Before I started dancing, I was writing. I used to write about everything, all the time. I can't quite remember when or why I stopped, but I did. My heart ached at the thought. Why had I given up on my dreams? What changed? I guess you could say "life got in the way," but why did I allow it to stop me?

Before I could ponder any further, I arrived at JFK about noon. Yay! Only 13 more waiting hours to go. I walked around for a while, hunting a power socket and a scale to weigh my bags. Eventually, I settled in on the spot on the floor near my ticketing area. The hours seemed to drag along. I watched as different groups of people came and went. There were tons of military guards with AK's walking around. I suppose everyone was still on edge from 9-11. I guess it's better to show any potential psycho with a hidden agenda, that the guards were not going to tolerate it, in hopes to make them change their mind. Luckily there were no crazies thus far...well except the darn airline!

Norwall Air really set me off today! I had called them several dozen times over the last few days. They specifically told me that my checked bag to be 20KG, my carry on had to be 10kg, and I asked about my backpack/purse, and she said "no bigger than 10KG". Why then, after that long bus ride and sitting in the terminal for 13 hours, did this lady tell me that my carry-on AND purse had to be 10kg COMBINED!!!!???!!! Talk about being livid. I was beyond angry. It cost me $65 at the gate, then when you get past TSA you can pretty much purchase whatever you want in the duty-free area. They could have let me have my carry on, primarily after I worked so hard to ensure it was 10kg. 65 dollars for a 12kg bag. I was extremely aggravated, but I wasn't going to allow them to have any more of my energy. I paid the bill and moved on.

Once I got past TSA, I wandered around for a bit running into the person I was standing behind in line during check-in. He's from the south of France. We had a delightful chat. We spoke about my adventure, the food differences that I am going to experience (Lord help us all), the conflicts with the Muslims and the French and, of course, we ate. He seemed like a very insightful man, who looked to be in his late 30's, mid-40's and had intriguingly sharp eyes. I wanted to ask him to speak only to me in French, but I thought that would be weird since I stopped speaking French back in my 6th year of school. I don't know why I felt strange, I was going to my people, but I felt like such an outsider that I stuck to English.

After our meal, we heard the announcer call our gate. I took a deep breath, scanned my ticket, and found my seat on the place. "Breathe," I whispered to myself, "When you wake up, you will be in Paris!"

4

I've arrived

I woke up exceedingly excited and nervous. Somehow, even the air felt different here. I found my way to the immigration line, which was exhaustively long. After the Dominican Republic told me that I could not enter the country, I'm always nervous about immigration at airports. You see, I had four suitcases and a carry-on with me. I had been in Nashville working on a project and was now off to D.R. to explore. I lived in Santa Monica. It was going to be impossible to drop my luggage off back in Santa Monica and then fly to D.R. …so I took it all with me. Apparently, to them, that meant I was trying to "live" in their country without telling them.

The lady was an obtuse jerk, to say the least. She said, "I saw your Facebook and website" with a less than pleased tone. What an ogre, for no reason at all. There isn't anything inappropriate on any of my pages. She seriously needed to go on a holiday and remove the stick from her arse. She also hinted at the fact they thought Derek was selling me off. I was furious, but I was totally over it. I tried filing a complaint like these people tell us to do, but it's a total farce. They know that no one is actually going to get back to us, that is why they won't accept an email. I had no choice but to return to the states. Feeling exhausted and frustrated, I decided to go Miami, and I found a few exciting things to do there.

My, somewhat rational, fear of immigration quickly subsided when immigration smiled, checked my passport, and said, "prendre plaisir," which is French for "enjoy". I walked down what felt like a forever corridor and climbed on to a moving pathway. I was startled by the rising of the platform. I clearly was not prepared for that, as I started sliding backward and trying not to fall over.

It was time for the frightening third part of traveling, the dreaded "did my luggage make it" moment. I stood there for what felt like 40 minutes, just waiting. At last, there they were, coming down the conveyor belt. "Thank God," I thought as I grabbed my hefty bags. Losing my luggage would have been pure hell. I also ran into Frédéric, the person from the luggage counter back in NYC. He offered to guide me to the train to get into Paris, and then he offered to see me to my destination; such a kind man.

Up and down the stairs, we went. We climbed eighteen staircases and rode four trains to get to Place du Commerce. At one point, a guy helped carry one of my bags. He didn't even ask, just grabbed it, took it to the top and set it down. As fast as the panic set in, so did relief. I wasn't sure what he was doing, but I am grateful for his help. After almost two hours, we climbed to the top of another staircase, and there we were, Place du Commerce.

Place du Commerce was surrounded by shops, obviously, and a cute little park. Some of the buildings were older, but those are my favorite. Frédéric and I stopped by a quaint café for a drink. I had suddenly realized that I hadn't had a bite to eat all day, but down and right to my head, the wine went. I felt myself getting the giggles very quickly, and I became increasingly talkative. It wasn't so great since booking.com failed to cancel a reservation and was trying to charge me for it. I had to call them in my current state and fuss with them. I was frustrated but not wholly. It felt kind of impossible to stay angered. It must have had something to do with my surroundings...and I am sure the wine helped too.

I met my host, Mathieu. He was a tall, scruffy man. We chatted about my journey to get here, and then he opened his kitchen window. My heart lurched. There it was, but not nearly close enough to satisfy my craving. Right away, I went to get dressed for the day and venture off, but first Mathieu and I had to grab food for the night.

We went to a small, produce store. The grocery markets in Paris were much different than the ones back in the states. There isn't one big store, you have several little shops where you get the specific thing you want. For instance, there is the produce market, the butcher, and the cheese shop. All to which we went. As the butcher cut a few slices of thick bacon, my mouth watered. I knew I needed to stop and eat, but I was also too excited to focus.

After shopping, I stopped back by the flat and grabbed my umbrella...something told me it might rain, and I wanted to be careful. Though it was just water, I wasn't in the mood for my hair to get wet. I grabbed my umbrella, then off I went. Mathieu provided me with some directions, but I think my brain glazed over from excitement because I suddenly couldn't remember them. Nonetheless, I set out to find my Eiffel Tower. I couldn't believe this was happening. I crossed a street and ended up on a dirt road, basically running into a massive group of runner's path. I wasn't sure why they were running, but it appeared to be an organized event. A tall, mysterious man in a suit spoke to me. He didn't speak English, but that was quite alright. We chatted for a few moments when I suddenly felt a chill go down my spine. I turned to looked up and there it was, my Eiffel Tower.

I was overrun with a great mixture of excitement, joy, happiness, and awe. I couldn't believe that I made it. I couldn't believe I was in Paris! I briskly walked to get into the queue for security. Once through I was literally under the Eiffel Tower! It was terrific, but, of course, that wasn't enough for me. I climbed and I climbed, for what felt like a good 30 minutes worth of stairs, stopping on the "hips" of the tower. The view was amazing, but I wanted to get to the top. I got in the queue that took an hour to open, then I stepped into another queue, finally boarding the lift.

Moments later, the lift's doors opened, and I stepped out. I saw a set of stairs, and I climbed those to have a good look around. The view was to die for, and I probably would have, if the net weren't there to prevent us from falling over the edge. I couldn't resist trying to look over it and see all that I could. The river was so mesmerizing. I didn't take notice that it had begun to rain on me. I was on top of the Eiffel Tower, and this was my heaven on earth.

After a couple of hours, the weather turned chilly, so I decided it was time to leave this magical place and, finally, get some food. I went down the lift and on to a second one where I met Oscar. Oscar worked at the tower. He too was a tall, dark, handsome, yet mysterious looking, man. Oscar complimented me, and we made small talk about my trip for a few moments. It was strange, we were in a lift full of people, but he did not look away once. His eyes were mysterious and dark. I sensed Oscar was trouble, but I gave him my card anyways. When I told him that I was thinking of returning to the tower to see it lit up at night, he said, "J'espère te voir bientot." Seeing that my suspicions were correct, I smiled and walked back to the flat.

My journey back was interesting. I had no clue where I was, but I could hear music, so I followed it. I followed the music into a building where people were dancing. Unfortunately, it was a private party that I had just crashed. I felt embarrassed, to say the least, and I continued my journey back to the flat. Only after circling the street twice, did I finally find it. Getting into the flat wasn't easy, either. It had a rather unique type of key, and for some reason I just wasn't, apparently, turning the key hard enough. Once I got in, I chatted more with Mathieu, and we decided it was time to cook and drink wine.

We created an exotic pasta dish that we made up as we went along. It had onions, garlic, ham, and pesto sauce in it. We added noodles and cherry tomatoes as we drank a couple of glasses of red wine and ate lots of bread slices. Bread is literally life. It was so crunchy on the outside, but the inside was warm and fluffy the way French bread ought to be. After supper, we discussed politics. Mathieu was quite intuitive. I appreciated that. He also wanted to know more about me, so I showed him my Facebook. I showed him photos of my mother and her mother and my little brothers. He also saw pictures of my work and my charity work and seemed to be impressed. Mathieu then showed me to an essential site. It was a website for college and work. It is where I could study, and the government would pay me while I studied, making it possible that I could stay here in Paris. I hadn't truly realized what I was considering. I hadn't made a plan, but the universe was urging me forward, so it seemed.

I won't lie, it sounded perfect to me. My heart yearned at the idea. A life in peaceful Paris...that could, very well, be my Paradise. I tried going to bed but I couldn't, so instead, I went for a walk remembering that I wanted to see the Eiffel Tower with its lights on. I journeyed back to the town only to see they'd turned the lights off. I was too late, but it was okay...I was still in Paris. I walked the night's streets, allowing myself to take it all in. This place, it feet so good, much like how Puerto Rico felt...but better. What was happening?

It was approaching 3 am, and I knew I should be in bed. I climbed in and began to drift off. I thought to myself, "I can't believe that I am in Paris, I can't believe that I climbed the Eiffel Tower." Realizing that I had accomplished one of my biggest desires, to leave the states and venture home, I couldn't help but smile. I had always hoped to venture off, but honestly, I wasn't sure I'd ever be able to. It was typical that people who grew up the way I did, didn't often see the outside of their environment. I was determined to change that...but first...sleep.

5

I QUIT!

It wasn't a dream. I woke up in Paris! Last night was fantastic, like a fairy tale almost…except I didn't lose a shoe and there was no prince involved. Walking the streets of Paris was a perfectly peaceful way to end my evening. I needed that moment of peace because all hell broke loose this morning.

After oversleeping, I checked my account, and there was a $7.41 USD balance on it! I called the bank, and they said all of the transactions I made in the USA they had to charge internationally. I was so frustrated. You would think if I purchased it online in the US that it would show me the full final cost in USD…but no. So all of that budgeting I did was for nothing. "What the fuck," I thought, what was I going to do? I couldn't possibly survive off $7.41 for an entire month! As frustrated as I was, it was also my fault for not double-checking as the transactions were being processed. How could I have been so foolish? It was just then, that it was raining. It was as if the weather was aware of my mood. The panic quickly started setting in. Why did I think I could do this all on my own without substantial savings? I called Jared, my friend back home, and told him to take my speaker box to the pawnshop then transfer the funds to my account. I was grateful that I held on to some of my things that carried a value.

Even though I had sorted the problem, the dark cloud was still looming over my head. I couldn't believe this was happening. My irresponsibility was about to put me into a perilous position before the trip could really get started. Just as I was about to give up for the day, give into the rain, and go to sleep, a boy named Scott messaged me asking to venture off. Reluctantly, I agreed. I needed to get out of my head anyway.

Scott was a shorter but energetic guy. A speedy walker, who wore a yellow raincoat that reminded me of the Guy with the Yellow Hat from Curious George. We decided to go to Notre Dame and explore Paris together today. We took the Metro where I saw a food stand. I was famished, and my nose could smell something delightful. Of course, it was a donut and I gladly purchased one. You would have thought I'd never had a donut before. It was terrific. The donut was not overly sweet, yet, had a dusting of powdered sugar that blended perfectly with the fluffiness of the treat. As the taste of the donut danced across my tongue, I couldn't help but smile. Here I am in Paris, eating a blissful donut, headed to Notre Dame. Unfortunately, because of the late start, by the time we got there, it was closed. I still, however, took my photo in front of it.

The towers were glorious. Such incredible architecture. From there, we walked to the "love-locks". I had heard the stories of lovers each signing their name on a lock, then attaching it to the Pont Des Arts. I walked along the bridge, thinking of how many generations of love had been there on display. Over time, the weight of the locks created a problem for the bridge. They were removed, and later relocated in

2015. Though this did not stop the lovers, they found other places to display their symbols of affection, some considering it to be good luck. Perhaps, one day, I would return and post my own lock.

We ventured past the Louvre Museum. It was massive. As much as I wanted to, there was no way we could see it all in one day, so we didn't even bother. Instead, we walked through its garden and headed for the Eiffel Tower. As we strolled through the garden, there were all these fantastic statues. I was enthralled by them. I tried picturing myself as one of them, blushing at the thought. I've been displayed in art galleries before, but never a statue. Though, now, it was something worth considering.

We strolled through the courtyard, and I saw the most perfect location to have lunch. I turned to Scott snapping images of me. He was a bit of an interesting person, as I learned when we chatted about life and politics. It seemed that everyone wants to know what the hell is going on in the USA and with the President. Trust me, those of us that live in the States would like to know as well.

We found ourselves walking down the "fashion district". At this point, neither of us had a clue as to where we were going, but we could see the Eiffel Tower, so we simply kept heading in that direction. I saw what appeared to be a little convenience store. "FOOD!" I thought, noticing how low my sugar was. I desperately needed food. I had yet to eat anything besides that little donut. Scott went in and declared that we needed a drink. Here I was thinking, "Oh, some juice might be nice." Nope. He asked, "Wine or beer?" and we settled on a bottle of Riesling.

Scott paid for the wine, and it blew my mind that they never asked either of us for an ID. In the states, you can barely lift the bottle without there being an ID check. It amused and intrigued me that we were able to walk outside, and all around the city, with a giant bottle of wine. As many officers we passed, no one questioned it. I looked around and noticed that many others were carrying their open bottles of wine around too. Incredible! Had that been the states, we both would have been cited for drinking in public and open container. By then, I started to think America had some serious work to do because France was winning my heart.

We walked past the Eiffel Tower and to another fantastic site called Jardins du Trocadéro. Up what seemed like a million stairs, I looked behind me and saw the most perfect view of the Eiffel Tower. I also smelled meat and bread. I turned around and saw two little food stands on opposite sides of the pavilion. I got in line, but it was taking forever, and I needed food immediately. I walked around to the other side, and there I met Jona.

Jona was a very tall, handsome man. His eyes were hazel, and he stood to be about 6'4. Standing in line, his eyes locked on me and I smiled, still a little preoccupied with the food. There were so many choices, but of course, I chose the panini with the most meat. It was enormous and only six euros, which is probably eight American, but I didn't care. I was starving. Much to my dismay, they did not take American dollars. "FUCK," I said to myself. Why didn't I change some money over?! Scott offered to get the sandwich for me, and I gratefully obliged. I hadn't had a panini until then. It's thick, fluffy bread held two slices of breaded chicken breast, tomato, and cheese. Jona offered to toast my panini, but there was something in the way he said the word *toast* that signaled to me that I was in the midst of

26

trouble. What was it about me that attracted such men? This trip was not about men, but that was all I seemed to have kept meeting. "Go on, have a little fun," I told myself, indulging Jona's advances.

He was truly French. The way his eyes looked at me, they screamed sex. He kept licking his lips and smiling at me. Every so often I would catch a little phrase he would say only in French, "Les choses que Je te ferais." I knew right away this man was trouble...but aren't all men? I suppose now is where I write about some crazy, Parisian sex-adventure, but no. We stood there, talking for a while about his life and the adventure I was on. He was a musician. Figures. He had a dream of traveling the world, playing his music. Moments later, he leaned in and whispered, "Anaís turn around, the light shines for you." I turned around, and there it was in all its glory, the Eiffel Tower, literally sparkling, I was completely enamored.

As I stood there staring at this amazing masterpiece, I began to think about my life. This is where I have wanted to be since I was four years old. Paris has always had my heart, but so much got in the way. So much pain I have endured...but here I was gazing at the Eiffel Tower at night, drinking wine. I thought that this day started out so horribly and I almost let it take me over. I almost didn't do anything because I almost let the pain win. I considered how often this was a recurrence in my life. Life would trip me up, and I'd allow the pain to consume me. It was incredibly unhealthy, and I knew it needed to change.

In that moment, I decided that I was giving up. I said to myself, "I GIVE UP," and I blew a kiss to the tower. I dedicated the remainder of this journey to locating my heart, which meant I had to start letting go of all it's broken pieces so it could heal itself. I gave up on the pain. I gave up on the chaos.

I gave up trying to live up to another person's standards. I gave up having a broken heart. I gave up having a lost spirit, and I gave up any and all things that did not bring me absolute peace and joy. There in front of the Eiffel Tower, in one of my favorite places in the world, I gave up "her". The me I used to be and never would be again. Tonight, I took my life back. I knew it would not be easy, but I knew there was a reason I was there, and I had to fulfill that purpose.

A while later, Jona and Scott asked me what the plans for the evening were. Truthfully, I really wanted to go dancing, but I could feel the wine going straight to my head, and that would not be so appropriate. I didn't want to be drunk in public with a lot of strangers just in case something happened and I needed to get away quickly. Jona enjoyed flirting with me. I noticed he was testing me to see how far he could go. As much fun as I thought he and I might have, I needed to keep my wits about me. He'd whisper, "Anaïs, tu es très jolie" when he thought I wasn't paying attention. I knew what he said, but I giggled, pretending to not. I don't take compliments very well. I become awkward, and it's always strange. He was sweet though…a very smooth talker, but I wasn't to be fooled.

I wasn't sure how to handle both Jona and Scott throwing flirtatious remarks at me. Eventually, I could tell Scott was ready to leave, which worked out because I started to feel uncomfortable, and I needed to check on my host. We said our goodbyes to Jona, but before I could leave, Jona asked to see me again. I enjoyed being admired. I decided that there would be no harm in a lunch or a nice walk, but boys like Jona cannot be told "yes" too soon, it goes to their heads (emphasis on the plural usage of head). I smiled and said, "Tu me verras encore /You'll see me again." He asked me to come tomorrow night, and I told him that I would think about it. Then I ran to catch up with Scott. On the way back, I noticed how badly my legs and feet were hurting, and I opted out of continuing the night. Scott was delightful, and I had a great time with him, I needed that adventure, but I also needed rest. When we arrived at my host's flat, I assured him that we would make plans another time and wished him goodnight.

As I laid there, trying to drift off to sleep, I looked at the clock, and it was almost 4 am again. "UGH," I thought, "so much for jogging in the morning." Still, I set my alarm in hopes that I would get up and I drifted off feeling such peace.

What is it about this place that has my heart soaring so much? Is it this place, or is it traveling in general?

6

c'est Paris!

I woke up this morning feeling surprisingly energetic. My host, Mathieu, wanted to hang out with some friends of his today, so I chose to get some work done, sorted my plans, and ate more pasta. I swear this pasta thing; I could totally get used to. A few hours later, we left and went to meet with Mathieu's friends. I had a feeling we would not be making it to Notre Dame today, so I put it out of my head. We stopped for them to grab some ice cream. Mathieu tried hard to coerce me into getting some, but I decided I was waiting until I got to Roma to get gelato. He still wanted me to try his, so I tried a tiny bit. I didn't really like it, but I smiled anyway. I'm not honestly the type to be rude...maybe that was part of my issue? I needed to become more confident in saying, "No."

We walked over to Jardin du Luxembourg, which was a delightful little park. There was an orchestra, unexpectedly, playing "I love you, baby." After offering our applause, we shortly moved on to sit along the pond in the center of the former Queen's Garden. It was quite busy. There was such a diverse group of people there and sitting around the pond laughing, talking, and drinking. It was so interesting to see none of the officers bothering the people as long as the people were not bothering anyone else. Something that had become foreign in the States - unfortunately.

Earlier today, I spoke with a few travel associates on one of my travel apps. Today I was going to meet with Laurent...if he could find me. I sat in the Garden with Mathieu and his friends for a while before I realized my wi-fi was off. Mathieu remembered that he had hot-spot, so I was able to bounce off of it to message Laurent, just as he was about to leave the area. He said he saw me, but was not sure it was me, and I was surrounded by other people, so he was not sure if he was intruding. He clearly was not since we all were just hanging out, so I told him to sit with us. I was immediately intrigued by his energy. Laurent was extremely tall...then again I am only 5'7". He had reddish hair, fair but tanned skin, a great smile, and eyes that seemed to tell more than his lips probably ever would. We all exchanged our political opinions, then went to find a Grec to eat. What I, basically, would call a "French burrito". It was surprisingly pretty tasty. It was tender lamb or chicken marinated in spices only to be roasted on a vertical spit, and then shaved off in chunks and stuffed inside a crepe. Then, a fistful of fries makes its way inside the epic sandwich-type snack, followed by the usual: tomato, onion, eggs, lettuce (eggplant for those who are willing). It was massively messy, super filling, and overall delicious.

I was a little annoyed because Mathieu's friend brought along two other friends and one of the guys, Uric, was extremely full of complaints. I understood he wanted "French food", but come on, dude! I wanted to go to Notre Dame, and we weren't getting to go there so if I wasn't going to complain because he wanted to sit around for hours, he should not have been complaining that we were eating where someone else wanted. That is the "trouble" with traveling with friends sometimes. There is always that one in the group, but when he wasn't complaining, his personality was tolerable.

We found a small park and sat to talk some more. I noticed there were military-style officers with AK's walking up and down the street. I was not used to that, but Laurent assured me that they didn't really bother people, so I should not worry. He and I discussed more politics. He wanted to know how I felt about guns, having coming from America, and seemed somewhat surprised by my response. I suppose I don't have a "typical American" viewpoint on life. I am both liberal and conservative. I don't fit into just either box; I prefer it that way. I explained to him that while I strongly believed in my right to bear arms, I felt as such came the responsibility to those arms. I believe in background checks, formal training, and accountability.

A while later, Mathieu stood to say they were leaving and put me on the spot. He looked at Laurent asking, very bluntly, "Are you guys going to hang out and party?". I was mortified. I, literally, stood there frozen. Laurent and I hadn't been flirting. We were just having a civil conversation. Laurent looked at me and said, "Sure." I felt so awkward. Why did Mathieu do this to me? I could feel the burning redness in my cheeks and was trying hard to hide it. Mathieu and his friend walked away, and Laurent looked at me, smiling. "Are you sure this is okay. I feel put on the spot." I asked him still feeling embarrassed. He laughed and told me to come with him. He wanted to show me Notre Dame at night. We set off continuing our conversation about politics and life. When we arrived, I couldn't believe how amazing it was. There is just something about the architecture in Paris that touched my soul. I suppose it's somewhat bittersweet considering very, very poor people built those buildings, but they are stunning, to say the least.

We walked around, marveling at the Notre Dame, then over to the river to sit for a while. It was pleasantly calming. There were several boats that took people around on tours. The walkways were two different sizes. One was very large, like twice the size of a sidewalk and the other (where we were sitting) was half the size of a sidewalk. We sat on the edge of the walkway, hanging our feet over and talking. We discussed everything from why I am on this adventure to his heart, my home (USA), his home (Tunisia) and how he feels about his recent break-up. It was nice having an actual conversation with someone and I was enjoying his company.

While we were watching the riverboats, Laurent stood up and said, "I am taking you to see the most perfect view of Paris, let's go!" I smiled and went with him. I had no clue where we were going, but I didn't care. Sure, I was following some stranger around Paris with terrible wi-fi, but something told me to just go with it...so I did. It was an adventure, after all. We rode the train, and we walked for a while...for a long while, actually. We then tried to board a lift, but my ticket was not working. Laurent gave me a look and said, "You're tiny...climb under." I was so nervous about getting caught with the officer standing right there that I just kept giggling as we hopped onto the lift. Laurent was clearly amused by my dorkiness, and for once, I wasn't completely embarrassed.

We rode to the top, walked down the street, and voilà. It was a marvelous view of Paris. Many people still had their lights on, so it was absolutely splendid. Even the clouds went away, exposing a full moon and stars. I was in "paradise", however, I should have known something was stirring when I saw it was a full moon.

It started to get a bit chilly, so Laurent and I walked back towards the lift. Before we went down the lift, he reminded me that I wanted to go dancing earlier. Truth is, I didn't forget. When he said he didn't like clubs, I didn't want to seemingly force him into going. I told him I was game to still go, and we went into a nearby Irish Pub.

The pub was pretty full already, and it was only about 10 pm (22:00). We went to the bar to get drinks, but it seemed like the bartenders couldn't see us standing there in front of them. Feeling a little risqué, I perked my boobs up, leaned over the bar and said, "beer, please." Right away, we got service. It's rather sad and yet quite amusing, the power of a pair of boobs.

After we got the beer, Laurent kept trying to get me to dance, but I needed to warm up to the music and wait for the right song to come on. Not to mention, I was genuinely distracted by the fact that the beer looked green. He kept telling me it was just the light, but I was still staring precariously at the beer. The beer itself had such an awful aftertaste. I kept trying to get Laurent to finish it. We shared it for a bit, but at the halfway marker of the glass, we both gave it up. The aftertaste was just too much to bear. It was perfect timing because "Shape of You" by Ed Sheeran was playing and it got me moving. Then, "Despacito" by Luis and Daddy Yankee roared through the pub's speakers. It took over my body, and I was in another world for at least three songs. I hadn't even noticed that Laurent's hands were trying to "wander." When I did realize it, I made him put his hands on my hips, and I kept dancing with him, not realizing that was only making the tension between us worse.

While we were talking on the pathways, I found myself staring at his lips thinking, "You should kiss me right now." but of course we ladies never say that stuff out loud. He must have been having similar thoughts because when we were staring at the city's lights, he kept his hand on my back and kissed me on the cheek. It was sweet, and I put it quickly out of my mind as soon as he did it. I try not to read into too many things, but there we were on the dance floor, my place where I let loose and get lost. Laurent spun me around to face him. He wanted me to look him in the eyes. I felt like the room was on fire, and I knew trouble was brewing. I separated our bodies and started dancing a few steps away from him with my eyes closed. I was slowly going into my zone. Unfortunately, my "zone" was now being split between being in Laurent's arms and the dance floor.

He spun me around again, this time having my back to him and his arms around my tiny waist. He, ever so smoothly, kissed my cheek and very, dangerously, slowly made his way to my neck. I could feel the fire in my veins and the temptation crawling up my spine. The more we dance, the more the tension rose. He leaned in for a kiss, but I knew what would ensue if I started down that path, it was too soon. I merely giggled and said "not yet" then kept on dancing. Our bodies in sync with each other, with every beat, he tried again. I laughed and said, "you are bad" trying to wiggle away, but not truly wanting too. He whispered in my ear, "I can be very bad" simultaneously, latching onto my neck before I could take a step back. The chills went through my entire body. For a moment, everyone in the room disappeared. Buttons were being pushed, and tension was at an unprecedented height. I pulled away firmly, telling him that we needed to go outside and cool off. I had to get out of there, I couldn't think straight with the music playing and with Laurent's hands on me.

We walked back to the spot where you could see the city lights. I looked out at them in complete awe. I had lost focus on Laurent. Paris truly was winning my heart. I stood there with a smile on my face feeling complete bliss, and I let my guard down. Before I could think the next thought, He grabbed me by my hips and kissed me. This time…I didn't stop him. The fire in my veins was now in my entire body. With every kiss, passion crept up my spine. He had found my weakness, and he knew it. Every time he kissed my neck, my back arched. He began to nibble and bite. The harder he did it, the more I purred. I thought to myself, "Did I plan this?" Truth be told, I kind of wanted him to kiss me when he kissed me on the cheek or when we were sitting on the river. I would try to pull away from his lips, but he'd only go back to my neck; oh, how I adore neck kisses. It began to get intense, I started clawing his back, and he lifted me in the air, wrapping my legs around his body. He pulled at my top while he was biting my neck. I arched, purred, and clawed his back. We hadn't paid any attention to the fact that at least 15 people were sitting on the stairs watching us. It took everything for me to pull away, but I did.

We went for another walk, but as soon as we got down the street, and away from peering eyes, we were at it again. We didn't even make it down the flight of stairs. Laurent's mouth made its way to my breast. Aggressively holding on to my waist and sucking firmly, yet gently enough not to hurt me on my nipples, I purred with delight. He put my hand on his pants, and it only made things worse. I enjoy turning others on. In fact, it is quite a turn on for me to know that I can turn that person on. I wrapped my hands around him, craving for more than a touch. He whispered into my ear, "Do you want me?" A managed to moan out a "yes" as he was kissing along my collarbone. The moment he heard "yes," he firmly pressed his body against mine and bite the right spot on my neck. My legs wanted to buckle under me. They must have, because he grabbed my waist and pulled us even closer together. Our hands searching each other's bodies, exploring almost every inch. Had it not been for the voices we heard approaching us, we probably would have stood on those stairs making out for another two hours.

Thankfully, people were approaching the area we were in distracting me enough to pull away. We walked down the stairs then down the street where we found a bench to sit on. Laurent lifted my chin, our lips meeting yet again. "Do you want to stay at my place tonight? I am not so far away," he asked me still caressing my back. I leaned forward to look him in the eyes. What was happening? I don't even know this boy yet here I am kissing and groping him. Sure, he was sweet while still gentle and aggressive in all the right ways, but what was this? Nothing, that's what it was, and that is what it would remain...at least for tonight.

I smiled and told him that as much fun as that would be, I still had morals for myself that I needed and wanted to keep firm too. He smiled and said, "Okay." Grabbing my hand and leading me on another walk, I could tell he was disappointed. In many ways, I was too, but I just could not go back on the vow I made to myself. If I crossed that line now, I would be destroying any progress I had made.

As we continued our walk, I could smell food. It was as if none of the making out ever happened. My brain went straight into "snack-attack" mode. We went hunting to see what might be open and we found a place that also happened to be in the strip club central of Paris. After we got our food, I had the idea of finding the Moulin Rouge before I left Paris. Laurent decided we were going to see it right then. We walked up and down the street, and then he said, "Turn around." There it was!! Mind you, it was pretty late, so the lights were off, but there it was. I imagined Satine sitting in the golden elephant, casually attempting to seduce the Duke, like she did in the film.

We continued our walk for a while longer, walking both sides of "strip club central" then I looked up at the sky. "Is the sun coming up? What time is it?" He laughed and informed me it was 5:30 am, so of course, it was the sun beginning to rise. It was getting chilly, and we both were getting rather sleepy. Laurent went to find a car to rent to drive me home since the train was going to make me wait another 30 minutes and he didn't want that. After finally locating one, we made our way back to the flat I was staying at.

The early morning streets of Paris were still pretty quiet, It was beautiful. Once we approached the flat, I hugged him and thanked him for the wonderful adventure. As I attempted to step out of the car, he pulled me back, and the kissing began again. On for another 5 minutes, hands began to "explore" again. "Grrrr." I thought. The kissing was getting more and more passionate from us both, so much that I had to come up for air and separate us for a moment. "Are you sure you don't want to come back with me?" he asked. I stared into his dark eyes, I had a feeling he was trouble right away, but I was enjoying the danger that sparked in his eyes. I was enjoying this, but I knew that it was all too swiftly happening. As much as I didn't want to, I knew I had to get out of that car immediately if I ever wanted to see him again, I couldn't allow things to go any further than they already had. The "runner" in me was too strong, and "this" would be over before it even began; the memory would be tainted. The sad truth is, he wouldn't have the slightest clue either. I could have given in to my dark side and bed him…then I would, undoubtedly, disappear…it's what I do, sadly. Oh, but I was so enjoying myself. I took a second to consider the reality of my potential actions. I mean, I was thousands of miles away from home. Who was to say we'd even see each other again or even speak again after this, anyway? I was slowly talking myself into it as he put my hand in his pants again. I purred with desire, but detached myself, reluctantly. No! I couldn't let it go further…not yet.

I smiled and gave him a deeply firm yet lingering kiss…then I said, "Get some rest darling." and I forced myself out of that car. When I reached my room, I saw that it was 6:30 in the morning! Had I, Anaís, just spent almost 18 hours with this boy wandering through Paris…among other things?!?! Who am I? I suppose that is what I came to Paris to find out…

7

I'm alive...I think

The next morning, I took some much needed "me" time. I woke up at 1 pm even though I was planning to wake up at 9 am and go to Notre Dame. Laurent messaged me to let me know he made it home, but I had passed out shortly after getting into bed. I responded back to him and began to get dressed for the day. I finally made it out the door at half-past 4. I wandered around for a while, then I made my way to the Eiffel Tower to relax on the green. It was so peaceful lying there on the ground, looking up at the tower. I tried to imagine myself living there. I couldn't help but smile. Every morning I would wake up for an early jog. Mid jog, I would stop in at the corner cafe for an egg croissant (or something for breakfast), a double shot of orange juice, a fruit cup, and some tea. I'd make my way to the center of the green, where I'd find a bench to have my morning picnic in front of the Eiffel Tower as the sun was rising. I would gratefully enjoy the fresh, crisp, morning air, loving the fact that I was alive and in my favorite place in the world.

I shook my head and smiled, almost dozing off wrapped in

my fantasy. The sun felt warm on my face. It was a beautiful day. I sat up and checked my phone for messages. I sighed to myself, seeing that I had several. I didn't feel like being bothered, but I told someone we would meet since I had missed him the previous day. His name was Karl. Karl was a somewhat shorter, much stockier guy. He had cool blue eyes, and if I had to guess, I'd say he was in his 40's.

We walked along to his apartment, which was a pretty decent flat. Up four sets of stairs that led to a wide-open unit with tons of natural light, we entered Karl's flat. The kitchen was quite small...for me, that is. Not the type of space where 3-4 people would be in there at the same time, but most places in Europe were shaped like that unless there was an open floor plan. I didn't go further than the living room. It was a large room, very modernly furnished. It all seemed to fit him well. I felt very awkward being there. I'm not exactly sure why, since he hadn't given me a reason to feel the way I did, but I was anxious to get out of there.

After about 30 minutes or so of us charging our phones, we stepped out to stroll the city. We walked to where Napoleon was buried, and we crossed over the Pont du Alexander III too. It was stunning. There were a few little sculptures on it and attached to the front of it. They were dressed in gold, and when the sun shined on them, they seemed to gleam. We took a few photos then walked around the bridge. Literally, almost a circle. I started getting that feeling when my sugar is too low. My knee and leg aches were beginning to catch up with me, and I knew it was time to get back to the flat. Karl showed me a pretty cool tower that had something to do with the Russians, and I saw the place again where Princess Diana died. Before I could allow myself to get sentimental, I heard music in the close distance. Upon getting closer, I saw it was two actual people singing Opera! Their sound was so fantastic. I don't think I've ever heard anything like it. I was genuinely impressed; a golden harmonious sound that was a decadence to all ears nearby.

We shortly arrived at a crossroad, where if we went left we could go to his place or if I went right, I could find my way back to the flat. I chose to go right. Karl wanted to grab dinner, and it sounded like a nice gesture, but something was telling me to go back to the flat. My instincts were freaking out, and I wasn't sure why I just knew that I needed to leave. I took a slow walk back, mainly slow because I kept getting lost, though I didn't bother to panic. Usually, I would not be so calm, but for some reason, I didn't mind being lost in Paris. Strangely, it already felt like home to me.

When I arrive back at the flat, Mathieu was home playing with his coffee machine. He looked like a kid in a candy store. Mathieu asked me about Laurent. "Did you see him today?" he smoothly questioned. I smiled and answered, "No, I went to the Eiffel Tower and for a walk." I tried changing the conversation, but Mathieu wasn't going to allow it. He asked me if I would see him again, but I honestly wasn't sure. Yes, we had some fun, but what would happen the next time we saw each other? Would we go on as if nothing was happening or would we go back to pressing those ever so dangerous buttons?

I didn't tell Mathieu what went on, but he continued to push the subject. "Didn't you have fun with him? He seemed like a good guy. You spent almost all day with him, yes?" I thought back to the previous night's incident and grinned. "He's cool. I don't know, we will see.", I replied. Mathieu and I discussed sex, and I attempted to explain my position on it, but he just couldn't understand it.

I didn't want Mathieu to know I just made out with this guy I had only just met. For some reason, I started semi-wishing it hadn't gone on. I tend to do this. I joke with my friends about it too. I say, "I am a vampire dominatrix with morals." Completely screwed up, I know, but it describes me best in my mind. I like pushing buttons, I like the clawing phase, and it absolutely turns me on to know that I am turning someone else on, but I don't want to experience that with most, many or several people. If I even try, I start to feel guilty because I know it will never work for very long. I'll get bored and disappear. Part of what "works" for me is the absolute attention we give to one another and that fact that we are "each other's." I absolutely look forward to getting married one day because we will be best friends, business partners, and 100% lovers. It takes for me to be physically, mentally, and emotionally turned on to ever cross that line with a person, I can't just hook up. Everything I like, want to do, and want to try...I will try with them, and it will be...my Paradise.

Mathieu laughed and said, "No, if I hold a girls hand all day, she will hold my penis all night." Truth is, what he was saying about it being "human nature that we become attracted, fuck, then go back to what we were doing before" is how many people view sex. "Sexually Free" is what they're called. That is okay...for them. It is not what I desire. The trouble is...it was never a question of whether or not I wanted him. It was always, was I going to allow myself to have him? We'd just met, spending much of the afternoon and evening together. When we initially connected to hang out, I simply was interested in meeting new people. I had no idea what would ensue only hours later. I enjoyed every moment of our time together. When we were talking in the park about politics, I was mentally stimulated. When we sat along La Sein and spoke of our different experiences with life, love, and learning...I was emotionally stimulated. When Laurent showed me the Sacre Coeur, and we talked of my obsession with mythology, the stars, and the moon, I was spiritually stimulated. And when we were dancing in the pub, I was physically stimulated. So it only made sense that our lips would eventually find each other.

The desire was there, and the temptation was high. I wanted to go with Laurent. I wanted to allow him to take control of my body. From the pub to the balcony, to the stairs, and on to the park...I wanted to close my eyes and just let go. I wanted him to kiss me when we were by the river. And when he kissed my cheek at Sacre Coeur, I wanted it to be my lips. I felt myself needing to be distracted by something other than him, that's why when we were at the pub, I tried being distant and getting lost in the music...but it was too late. I was becoming wrapped up in something deliciously dangerous, and I didn't want to stop. I wanted more. I wanted to stay in the car...but I couldn't...I just couldn't allow myself to cross that line. If I hooked up with Laurent that night, I would have never spoken to him again. Since there wasn't a foundation formed, it would have just been an adventure hook up, and I would never see him as more than the guy I picked out in Paris. No one deserves to be treated that way, which is why I walked away, resisting the temptation to sit on his face.

I thought about going for another walk before bed, but I was exhausted. I decided instead to get some work done and plan my next day. One more full day in Paris...(sigh).

8

But...Paris?

I woke up late, again! Maybe today I did it on purpose. I was rather depressed that I was leaving Paris. I wasn't ready. I lay in bed, pouting for awhile. Why did I not plan more time in Paris? "This journey isn't over." I told myself. I pulled my butt out of bed and opened the window. It was 72 degrees and not a rain cloud in the sky. I looked over at my things and said, "Fuck it." I pulled out one of my dresses that I had yet to wear, and I got ready to enjoy my last day in Paris. I figured I would just end my night early and pack before I headed to the station. The sun was up, and I needed to be outside in it. I made plans to meet a new person for a little while, then I said, "Eiffel Tower tonight." I was going to for sure see those beautiful lights before I set out on the rest of this journey. I pulled out my heels and went strolling through the streets.

I felt absolutely fabulous. People were staring and smiling at me. You would have thought I was six feet tall, with how I was walking. I was doing my runway walk even though I was only going to the store and bank. I didn't care, though. I looked hot, and there was just something about being in Paris that made me feel amazing too. I walked past a rather expensive jewelry store, and I overheard someone say, "Wow, did you see her?" I smiled and kept walking. After I left the bank, I had to go back past that store, and I heard the person say, "There she is!" I stopped and looked down the street as if I were looking for somewhere. Truthfully, I just wanted to hear what they were saying about me. The girl in the store asked, "Who is she?" to the guy beside her who replied, "I don't know. She is stunning". An older gentleman joined the other two. Having walked past me from the street, he asked them if I were a celebrity, but the trio couldn't put their finger on it. I just couldn't help myself, so I turned and walked inside. They each greeted me, and I asked for directions to a nearby café then left with a smile on my face. It was nice hearing strangers speak kindly about me. I supposed when you are so hard on yourself, you tend to appreciate the occasional uplifting comment. It's when guys make sexual comments that things become awkward.

I went back to the flat to drop off some of my money, then I made plans with Oscar, the older guy from the Eiffel Tower on day one. He wasn't too far away, so I put my flats in my coat pocket and went towards the café to meet him. Oscar was a tall, slender, and older man. He too looked to be in his 40's. I remember when he and I first meet, he tried to compliment me. Oscar said, "Beyoncé?" not knowing that I hated to be compared to others. Nonetheless, I smiled and nodded to him. He said, "I think you are more beautiful than Beyoncé." Also, not realizing that putting down another female to uplift me wasn't flattering to me in any fashion. He asked the typical questions, "Are you visiting? Where are you from? What brought you to Paris?" It was a little weird because we were in a lift full of people.

Oscar and I walked towards the Eiffel Tower, but he didn't really have a plan, and neither did I. So, we just kept on walking. When we got towards the Napoleon Monument, I told him I'd already been in that direction. We turned left, and it hit me. My sugar dropped so low so fast. I assumed we would find a lovely café and sit around, but we kept walking. I asked, "Where are we going...is there a café?" He said, "Only a little further," but we crossed two large bridges and passed a bunch of shops. As we went down a rather savvy street, I began to feel weaker and weaker.

I took a seat and told Oscar that I needed to get back to the flat. He didn't seem too pleased. He showed me how to get back, but it was still a bit confusing. I never did pay enough attention to the Metro; I wished I had at that moment. He decided to take me all the way back to Place du Commerce. I was grateful, but I started to feel strange. I felt like I shouldn't be with him. Not like I was in danger, but like I just shouldn't be with him. It was very unnerving, so after I stopped to grab a sandwich, and we parted ways. There was just zero chemistry there, even for being friends, but that's life I suppose.

I went back to the flat and checked my messages. A guy named Adrien had requested we meet. I figured since it was my last night in town, why not hang out with as many people as possible. Adrien was not necessarily from France, but he was as French as one can get. When he picked me up, we drove around the block and went for a walk stopping at a patisserie. I purchased a "Pain au chocolat", which is basically bread with chocolate chips. It was heavenly. It was succulently buttered and loaded with dark chocolate chips. Inside was a delicate vanilla crème that seemed to bring the treat altogether. The first bite, my tongue began to dance, even my body wiggled a little. I was undoubtedly a fan of this treat. Adrien laughed, I suppose he'd never seen a girl dance because of food before, but there was a first time for everything. Unfortunately, he didn't have much time to hang out, so we walked back to the car and he dropped me off at my host's flat. He asked if we could hang out after 10: 00, but I told him I had to leave for the airport then since the underground would be closing at 1 am. He decided that he was going to take me to the airport so we could hang out some more. I was hesitant, but I agreed.

I went back inside to greet Mathieu. He was busy in the kitchen, so I went to my laptop. That is what was so cool about him…he didn't invade really. I mean sure he often asked inappropriate questions for the average person, but it didn't honestly bother me. If I didn't want to answer, I'd simply smile and change the subject. Mathieu watched as I vacuum-sealed my luggage. He couldn't believe that I'd traveled with so much, but this was nothing. Usually, when I travel, I have 4-5 suitcases with me. It's crazy sometimes, but I always feel like I need the items.

Mathieu began to ask his questions again about Laurent. I couldn't figure out why he was talking him up to me so much. He'd say, "Oh, he's a good guy. He hung out with you all night. You must see him before you leave. It's you're last night." I did think about seeing him again, but he told me he had to work, so I didn't bother. We chatted a little bit, but he was busy with his day and me with mine. I figured if he wanted to see me again, he'd say so…but Mathieu wasn't letting it go. I changed the subject to about me being sad that I'm going to be leaving to go back to the U.S. He laughed and said, "But no, you are staying. You and Laurent are getting married and poof you'll be here full-time." I couldn't help but laugh. "Seriously?" I thought. I dared to ask him a question. "So, explain to me how that works?" I didn't know what I was getting myself into. Mathieu said very plainly, "You are going to see him tonight, and you are going to kiss. Then he will ask you to marry him because he cannot live without you".

I laughed so hard then I fed into Mathieu's silliness. "OH wait. What if, just as I'm about to board, he comes running through the airport screaming 'Wait, you can't leave!" and he is having a hard time breathing from all the running, but he manages to say, "You can't leave." When I ask, "Why not?" He says, "Paris has great fashion, food, and Paris has me." Then he takes me in his arms and kisses me. The entire room claps and I hear, "Last call for flight 331 Paris to NYC." I look at him and say, "I'm where I belong." Mathieu then abruptly said, "...and then he takes you home, and you have crazy Paris sex." We both laughed. I gather we watch too many movies.

I went back to packing the rest of my luggage. I heard Mathieu say something about messaging Laurent, but I didn't believe that he'd actually do it. A few moments later, Laurent messaged me asking if I was looking for him. My goodness!! I couldn't believe Mathieu did that! I was a bit embarrassed, yet I couldn't be so much because if the shoes were on the other foot, I'd totally have messaged a girl for him. The problem is, I don't even know if I like the guy. Yes, we had some fun, but that's all it was...fun. I think I've become very detached to people and interactions. Most girls would have been 'over the moon' and wanting to text and talk, but as soon as the night was over...it was all over for me. There wasn't anything "lingering." Was this my fate? I felt like my humanity had been turned off, and I was just existing. How could I want someone so passionately, then it all turns off 48 hours later? I wondered if it was just something I was telling myself, so I would never get attached again, but is that a good way to live?

Finally! I was finished packing after two hours of silliness. I was preparing to walk to the underground when Adrien messaged me to notify me that he would be picking me up shortly. "Wow," I thought, "he's actually going to take me." I'm not sure why I was so surprised, but I was. Most guys...most people, don't keep their word, especially if it's not less than 5 minutes away. Even then, good luck in Santa Monica. It was a little past 11:00 when Adrien got to me. He, too, was shocked at the amount of luggage. I just kept thinking, "This is nothing." He apologized for being late then we went to my favorite place, The Eiffel Tower. I needed to see it one last time. I knew I'd be back on the 5th of June, but it'd only be for a couple of days, and it was so far away, I needed to see it before the rest of my journey.

We parked and climbed the stairs to the Place du Trocadero. Adrien had gotten hungry, so he went for a snacky. I was standing there staring at the Eiffel Tower when I heard a familiar voice say, "Hey, Anaïs." It was Jona! I felt terrible that I hadn't gone back to meet him that next night, but I was rather...tied up in a web of "messes". He seemed happy to see me. We talked for a bit, and I almost didn't see Adrien walk up. I told him about how crazy my week had been, and he encouraged me to keep working on my journey. We both seemed to pick up on Adrien's presence, so I smiled, and he went back to work. Adrien led me to sit on the stairs and talk. He asked me if I wanted a bite of his sandwich. It was called a "Croque Monsieur." I laughed so hard. "I'm eating WHAT?!" I asked, still laughing. It sounded like I was eating a *cock* Monsieur. We repeated saying it, mostly with me giggling as how closely the word sounded like 'cock'...as in I'm eating a mister's dick. I can sometimes be easily amused. Amid our hysteria, a guy walked up with a few bottles of wine. He wanted 20 euros for a cheap bottle of Rosé. I laughed and haggled with him a bit. I told him, "No way, 15. I can get the bottle for 8-12 bucks in a store down the road." He rebutted, "Okay, 18." But I held firm to my 15. We settled at 15 euros and Adrien seemed impressed. I laughed, telling him, "It's just the trick of the trade is all." as we "cheers'd".

A little while later, Jona walked over to us. I invited him to sit for a while, but I could tell he felt uncomfortable. I think he felt like he was interrupting a date, but Adrien and I just met and were just hanging out, though I did think he was rather sweet. We all talked about my upcoming travels, life in Paris, and what would I decide. We were laughing at the word "Croque" again when suddenly the sparkles on the Eiffel Tower shined. I immediately fell silent...and was in awe. It was amazing that something so simple, felt so magical. When the show was over, I smiled at the Eiffel Tower, blew it a kiss then set off for the airport.

I took a moment to stop by the Bataclan Theater, where the massacre from the terrorist attack happened. I said a little prayer and set a rose at the door. It's strange how something can affect you even if you are nowhere near the area nor were involved in any way. After a moment of silence, we got back into the car and set off again, this time for sure to the airport. I started thinking about when we were laughing at the word 'croque,' and I began to think about the Eiffel Tower shining again and I thought of Adrien and Jona. It's strange, they both want to be in America, and I want to be in Paris. This is where my heart has always been. This is where I needed to be, I was sure of that, but I needed to also complete this journey to ensure I truly felt that way.

London...here I come.

9

London

'There's a hole in the world. A great black pit. And it is full of people who are full of shit. And the vermin of the world inhabit it.'
– Sweeney Todd

This song repeated in my mind as I prepared for London. My heart was still longing for Paris, but my soul needed to complete this journey, and London was next on the list. The boarding was pure hell. Transavia is probably one of the worst airlines I'd ever encountered. The check-in rep told me it was fine to have my purse because my meds and passport was in it and it could go under the seat in front of me, but when I went to board, all hell broke loose. I asked the rep at the boarding gate to translate what the intercom said, and he dismissed me saying, "You can't have that. Only one bag."

I looked down at my purse, confused, and I informed him that inside my purse held my medications, my passport, and other vital documents. He didn't care. I requested to speak with a supervisor, and for 45 minutes he avoided me, refusing to assist me. Finally, after an hour of drivel over a purse, I paid 40 euro just so I didn't miss my flight, but not before I took a photo of the incomparable jerk. He thought he won, but it was far from over! There is a time and place for everything, so I handled it as best I could, but I had every intention on following up and going above his head. Often, it's not what the person says, but how they choose to say it. As if that wasn't bad enough, the engine was not functioning properly on the aircraft. The noises that echoed through the plane made the hairs on my arms stand. The moment the pilot announced that we were experiencing difficulties with the engine, my heart began to race. All my irrational flight fears seemed to attack me at once. Talk about freaked out. It was a terrible experience that I would never hope to repeat.

Two hours later, I finally arrived in London. I was very pleased and appreciative of my buddy Declan retrieving me from the airport, especially since it was two hours from London center. Feeling my sugar get low, we stopped to grab some breakfast then decided to go to Shakespeare's home! It took another two hours to get to Stratford-Upon-Avon, most of which I spent sleeping. Overrun with excitement, I felt my inner Thespian leap for joy the moment we checked in. Anyone that knows anything about me knows I positively adore Shakespeare. One of my favorite quotes by him is, *"Though she be but little, she is fierce."* I especially admired his unapologetic display of his work. I understood that he might have been a difficult person to work with, but aren't all the greats?

For me, Shakespeare was a beacon of hope and a force of faith. Back then, theater and writing were one of the most important acts we could do to express ourselves. I'd say it still is. It's fantastic how a movie, a poem, a book, or a performance can touch another person's soul, potentially impacting the rest of their life. We tend to connect through these moments, and I believe it's what brings us together. We tend to learn that we aren't alone in whatever we're feeling and that, in itself, is vital to our self-esteem and emotional stability. I'm delighted Declan took me there. It was bittersweet leaving, but I needed to get to London and get this next part started.

Declan and I drove throughout London. Traffic was awful, not that I really had to experience it. My body kept shutting down. I wasn't sure what the problem was, perhaps the lack of rest, but I kept falling asleep. He showed me some of the most important places in London then we went to get more food before going to meet my host, Michal.

Michal worked in the business district, but I couldn't exactly remember what his specific trade was. He was from Prague but had been living in London for a while. We went up on the roof so I could see the city area and get to know each other. It's always interesting when I meet a new host. I'm very much an introvert and found it slightly challenging to desire to hold long conversations. The roof had a perfect view of the Canary Wharf District. I was surprised at how modern London was. I supposed I had it stuck in my head that London was still cobble walkways and houses made of only brick. I don't think I ever paid attention in all the movies at how London was a European NYC, but it was indeed.

It was raining a bit, so Michal and I went back inside to drink more wine and chat. He was amazed to find out I knew anything about computers and tech stuff. It appeared very important to me that women allow themselves to be smart as well as attractive. It's so strange when people are surprised that I have a brain. I suppose that's because most of society wants us to be one or the other. I refuse to be stuffed into a box.

As Michal and I said our good-nights, I laid there thinking about it all. I want to be more than just another pretty face, and I want to encourage other ladies to embrace both of their sides because we CAN be beautiful *and* intelligent.

10

What does London have to offer?

Today I got up rather early so I could leave when Michal does. He showed me through the Canary Wharf, and we went our separate ways. I walked into the building that served tea, deciding to purchase a tea and a brownie. I giggled because my friend Joey would be giving me the "look" since I was starting my morning with sweets. I ate it with the delight of knowing that he would be displeased. I took a sip of my tea and YUCK! What on earth was this?!?!?! I opened the top and remembered that British people drink black tea and put milk in their tea. Immediately I found the sugar and 5 packets later, I sipped my tea happily. I walked outside, ready to set off on my adventure only to realize that I had no clue where I was going. I looked around to see if I could find help, but it was the morning rush. Thankfully a gentleman, who was working on a building, was able to give me directions to the underground. Though, when I found it, I felt even more confused. Apparently, you must have an oyster card and guess what? In most of Europe, they use Euros...not in England, they use pounds. I was pretty annoyed to be honest, primarily with myself that I had made such an error in not knowing what money to use. I should have known better but in the rush of excitement that has become this journey…I spaced. Graciously, the attendant permitted me to board without a ticket since it was my first time in London.

Sitting on the underground, I looked around at all the different people. Some seemed wealthy enough, and others not so much. One thing everyone had in common was they were all avoiding the traffic on the main roads. I wondered why Santa Monica hadn't invested so much into our public transportation system. It's quite a mess if you ask me. I felt really safe here in London, but not so much in Santa Monica or Chicago. Probably just a difference in culture.

When I arrived at Westminster, I walked to the right, out of the underground, and into "Big Ben". It looked much different than how it does when we see it in movies. I somehow thought it was a separate building in the middle of London, I suppose that is what I get for watching so much TV. This is why traveling is imperative to your growth. I get to see it for myself and form my own opinions from my personal experiences.

I walked around for a while and saw a cathedral. I didn't go in because I was trying to find Buckingham Palace. I must have wandered around for at least 2 hours before actually finding it. Getting lost had just become a part of the journey. I went to the Somerset house only for them to be seemingly closed for a special event, which was okay considering they moved the records department to Liverpool. From there, I found my way to Hyde Park, walked through the park, and wandered into the National Museum. It was exceptionally large and fascinating. I was able to personally see some of the greatest masterpieces from hundreds of years ago. It's safe to say that I was "totally nerding out." but looking at the Van Gogh was incredible. Many of the paintings were about Christ from the artists' perception. I think I spent an easy two hours walking around the whole place. The architecture was amazing, simply breathtaking, and I felt comfortable there.

After a bit later, I finally found Buckingham Palace. If you've ever seen a map of London, then you know I literally walked completely out of the way since what I was looking for was only a few blocks over. I took a few photos but was ready for Kings Cross Station. I got lost again. Go figure, right? I couldn't believe my phone was dying so quickly and I was tired of walking in circles, so I stopped the next person that walked past me to ask for directions. Much to my luck, he was going in the same direction, so we walked together. His name was Tim, and he was getting married very soon. He told me about his adventures that he and his fiancé went on and the adventures they were planning to go on. I love when men speak so openly about their loves. It, in my opinion, means they truly love them because they're not afraid to love them out loud even in the presence of a beautiful woman. I'm pretty excited about their life-long adventure even though I don't even know them. I suppose love makes me excited.

We passed the British Museum, and I told myself to remember to stop there again...but it didn't happen. We walked into Kings Cross, and I was again surprised. It didn't look at all how I expected it to look. I don't know why, but I expected to see...well, trains and such. That's what I get for being a Harry Potter nut. How did I not realize that London was going to be so modern? It's one of the most capitalized cities in Europe. I couldn't believe how ignorant I had been. I decided then, "I really need to get out more." I mean, even in "Potter", London was pretty modern.

Speaking of Potter, Tim took me to the Platform 9 ¾! He had to run to his train, but I was thankful he helped me find it. OMG, the Potter nut in me was flipping its shit! The store was precisely how I would expect it to be. They had a little of everything from every book. I loved the wands, but I opted to not purchase one. I was on a budget, and I needed to be careful, this was just the beginning of this adventure, and I didn't wasn't to run out of food money. I did find a key chain I liked. In Paris, I decided I needed tokens from my trips, and little key chains would be perfect. I picked one up and purchased it. There was so much to choose from, but I told myself, "No." I walked outside, and I just couldn't help myself. I found myself in line to take a "boarding" photo.

I listened to the kids and parents in line. It's incredible that such a fantasy was able to touch so many different types of people. I will be forever grateful for J.K Rowling. Her books were one of my escapes from my abusive childhood. There is something splendidly magical about a great song and a great book. Once I'm lost in it, it's like all of the troubles go away, even if only for a little while. I remember I used to sneak and stay up with a flashlight to keep reading. A good book will do that to you.

I got my photo then I heard a crash of thunder. Fuck. It was pouring again, I had no clue exactly how far I was from Michal's flat and of course my phone was dying, and my power bank was already dead. I made my way out into the rain and just started walking, hoping I was going in the correct direction. I saw a leasing office, and I asked to charge my phone for a moment. I literally only had a moment because they were closing, but I figured 8% was better than zero, so I didn't complain. I kept walking and made it to an underground station. I asked another person for directions, and they looked it up on their phone. I had a 2-hour walk ahead of me, and it was pouring rain...yay.

I just kept walking, hoping I was going in the correct direction. Whenever I could find someone without headphones on, I'd ask for directions and kept walking. It appeared many didn't have a clue even where they were. I laughed at the realization that we humans just walk around, bumping into each other and things randomly.

I had been walking for quite a while, and my leg was absolutely killing me. There was an extremely sharp pain shooting through my leg from my knee, but I couldn't stop, I had to get back. It was now dark and windy, but I kept telling myself to keep walking, that I would find it. My pants were soaked, I was freezing, and my sugar was dangerously low. I was so angry with myself. What was I doing out there? I should have taken a taxi or something. I know how quickly I get sick, yet here I was walking for 12 hours in the rain and wind. Just as I was feeling destroyed, God smiled on me...with a tavern of all places.

The George Tavern. I walked in slowly, not really sure what I was walking into. As I entered the Tavern, I was greeted by the owner and a few others. Everyone seemed rather warm in spirits, but that could have easily been the booze. I asked for directions to Canary Wharf, and they were shocked that I was trying to walk all the way there. After all, it was still another 45 minutes until I got there and 20 minutes from there to the flat. The owner looked at me and seemed to have taken pity when he found out I only had euros, not pounds, so I couldn't ride the underground. He offered me some tea and a meat pie. I smiled internally as "Ms. Lovette's Meat Pies" from Sweeney

Todd started playing in my mind. I looked at the pie curiously because I'd never had one before. It wasn't larger than the palm of my hand, so I popped it into my mouth. It really was just a meat pie! A giant piece of pork sat in the middle of it, surrounded by savory gravy and a flaky piecrust. I thought having these at a bar was a rather genius idea.

I sat at the bar, having a chat with the owner, and he introduced me to a few of his friends. Everyone seemed really content and calm. He handed me another cup of tea, and I just sat, listening to everyone talk and laugh. I discovered that the owner's mother really owned the place, and it had been in their family for hundreds of years. Some company wanted to tear it down and build apartments, so they held a rally to save the Tavern. I thought that was really inspiring and awesome; I'd totally rally to save my favorite bar. I looked around the pub, understanding why others loved it. It had an old-time charm that you just didn't find everywhere in London. Before I started off on my journey back to the flat, the owner invited me to come to listen to live music the following evening. I was certainly going to do that, especially after he'd been so kind to me.

About an hour later, I finally made it back to Michal's flat. I was soaked, frozen, and exhausted. My only saving grace was stopping in that Tavern for a while. I had left at 8:30 that morning and it was now a quarter to midnight. My legs were hurting so badly that I could barely move anymore. I got undressed, washed off the makeup and dirt, and collapsed onto the couch. Michal handed me a glass of wine, and before I knew it, I was ready to pass out…at least I thought I was. For some reason, I struggled to fall asleep, so I laid there with my eyes open thinking about the day. Maybe tomorrow would be better.

11

Oy!

I woke up so late today, almost making Michal late for work. I kind of felt bad for it, but it wasn't indeed my fault that I didn't hear my alarm. My knee stiffened so badly during the night. I hardly got any sleep due to the pain, but I was going to muddle through it and go to the library. I just couldn't explore today for 10 hours. I rushed to get dressed, and out the door we went.

I walked around the business district until I found the library. It was pretty large, and from the outside, it totally did not look like a library. I walked in and had a look around, still not positive I was in the correct location. Before I could reach the help desk, some guys started catcalling. Why do guys do that? Why not just politely introduce themselves? Do they honestly think they're going to get anywhere with "Hey, hey! Come have a chat with me." To be fairly honest, it's extremely annoying and makes me want to be a bitch to them automatically. Any guy catcalling is a complete coward with an extreme lack of class. Thus, I completely ignored the knob-heads and found the lift.

I'm sure my pain wasn't helping my mood. My knee pain had become excruciatingly painful, but anything strong enough to stop the pain was going to cause me to fall asleep. My leg was killing me. I quickly found a couch, then set up my chargers and laptop. Having a look around, I appeared to be in "Muslim county". This meant I was bound to find great food when it was time. I found it interesting how I grew up around people like them in Chicago and hadn't ever had an issue with any of them. I still don't. These extremists are really screwing up the world and when I say 'extremist' I mean ALL: Muslim, Christian and Atheist alike. Everyone is out to prove their point, and all they're really doing is hurting society. In my opinion, everyone that is an extremist is being a terrorist to good civilians. I'm so tired of it.

I opened my laptop, trying to get to work, but I was far too distracted. I started thinking about the States, my friends, my brothers, and HIM. Damn you, London! With your gloomy skies, got me thinking about everything I'm supposed to be clearing my mind from - but I couldn't help it. I wasn't really enjoying London the way I had Paris, and at that moment, I started to feel a bit alone.

I started to think firstly about my brothers. I wondered how they were. My mother's "ex" keeps calling me, but what could he want? I missed my boys so much. I hadn't heard from them since the start of the year - pretty much right before I cut mother off. I sometimes feel like I made a mistake, but I know in my heart that I did not. I needed to cut the feed-line to her chaos. I don't want to be anything like her, so the very first step was cleansing myself of her nonsense and the guilt for doing so by forgiving myself. For so long, I hated myself for allowing evil people to be in my world: Mother, Grandfather,

David…and HIM. I often felt like if I allowed them in and allowed them to hurt me…I must have wanted it, or maybe it didn't hurt that badly. I know that's not the truth, but when you are trying to heal and processing, your mind starts to play games with you.

Why do I do it? Well, that answer is simple. I think I can fix them. I made myself believe that if I could show them that there was good in them, then they would change for the better. In some instances, that may be true, but the problem I have been avoiding is admitting to myself that perhaps there was no good in them and the good I thought I saw was only there because I wanted it to be so badly.

I looked out of the window at the little store across the breezeway. Immediately my tummy growled, but I couldn't bear to walk there then back up to where I was stationed. Besides, what if someone took my seat? Rather than deal with the possibility of all of that, I stayed put, taking out a snickers bar I had stored in my backpack's pocket and ate it. "Mmm," I thought, but I truly wanted something with meat in it. I started having crazy random thoughts like, "What if all the stores closed, how could I get my meat?" I decided I needed to learn how to accurately track and hunt, and I needed to try different meats since I doubt chicken and beef will always be so accessible if the world came crashing down. I laughed at my thought process. Hunger makes you think and do weird things, but so does love.

I started thinking about this entire London trip. It was not as sweet as France had been. It's been raining nonstop, I hurt my knee pretty badly, and I've gotten hardly any sleep. Maybe I should have spent more time in Paris. I did enjoy Paris very much. I don't know what it is about the place, but it felt like spiritual magic to me - even just sitting in front of the tower felt great. I knew it was too early to start complaining about this journey; after all, London was only my second stop. I still had five more places to visit. I told myself, "No great adventure ever was completed without a bit of a storm in it." I decided that London was merely my thinking place, after all, the entire trip couldn't possibly be completely fantastic…if it were, what would I learn? Maybe London was so chill because I really needed to think about myself, my life, and what I wanted.

I pretty much know what I want. It's just the process of getting it, and allowing myself to enjoy it. You see, I work very hard, and for some reason, that is never good enough for me. I always feel like I have to work harder and longer to deserve success. Maybe that's a part of the problem. I work so hard without really enjoying what I am working for. That can't be healthy. I mean, sure you need to work hard, but at the end of the day what are we working so hard for? When we die, we can't take any of our success with us. We tend to get tunnel-vision. "If I work hard and only focus on this for 15 years, I can retire and never have to worry about it at 40." But what happens if you die at 39? Was it all worth it if you've never allowed yourself to enjoy any moment of it? I suppose that's truly what some of this journey is about. I've got to stop being so hard on myself. I do outstanding work with my charity and within my career. Maybe it's okay for me to just relax a little bit. Perhaps I don't always have to be so "on top of things". If I am so busy looking forward to that end result, I will be missing all of the exciting things that occur along the way.

I then had to admit to myself that that is probably why I don't have a real interest in dating currently. The problem with the idea of building my empire then finding love is, well, that's just not how real love works. You can't just "find" it, it finds you whether you are ready or not. I often wonder if my work was one of the things that destroyed HIM and I. I know it was several other things as well, but I am only responsible for my shortcomings in the situation. Maybe it wasn't true love. I would like to think that I would know if the love of my life was standing before me and that I wouldn't allow work or other bullshit to stand in the middle of us, but that's not easy to state. There are tons of missed opportunities. We call those "the one that got away". Though the only one I feel that got away was the real me, and I was determined to find her.

That night, I fell asleep thinking about the woman I wanted to be when I was a child. I thought about all of the things I was trying to accomplish. I still couldn't believe that I gave up so many of my dreams. One day, looking in the mirror, I told myself, "You have a fresh start. It sucks your memories are gone, but there isn't a damned thing you can do about it, so get through it. This is your opportunity to find your Paradise." It was that night that I decided that I was going to go on this journey. To many on my social media pages, it just looks like I'm off on a holiday or something, but truthfully…this is probably the hardest thing I've ever done. I'm still accepting the fact that I dropped everything, everything I didn't truly need, and I took off to Europe. The Lord knows I needed this. I have this crippling fear that if I don't find what's missing now, that I will lose me forever. I don't want to live that way. So many people just exist daily, but few are actually living. I can't be another sheep in the herd. I need to find substance and value within my life, for myself. I am always there for so many, but this…this I needed to do solely for me, unapologetically.

12

My poor legs.

I woke up in sheer pain. I wasn't sure what was going on, but I had horrible shooting pains throughout my legs, and I struggled to walk. I decided I needed to find something nearby to explore today. I didn't have it in me to wander all over London again, at least not at 8 in the morning. I walked around the Canary Wharf area seeking food, then back over to the Dock London Museum. It was closed for another hour, so I waited on a nearby bench and enjoyed the little bit of sun that was touching my face. I found myself dozing off when I heard children voices signaling that the museum was open, and it was now time for me to explore.

I started at the very top and decided to work my way down. On the 3rd floor, it was all about the dock and the types of tools they used to work around the dock. Most of them back then were simply made of iron. I tried to lift a couple and saw how heavy they were. I guess the dock workers were really fit men. We don't really have intense manual labor anymore. Could that be why the world is either so skinny or obese?

I made my way through a corridor to the 2nd portion. It was

all about the slave trade. There's always been a desire of mine to hop into Dr. Who's tardis, so I could go back in time and really see where it all started, but let's face it, it would not be the most responsible thing. I'd think I would help prevent slavery, but would end up on a pyre for accidentally mentioning the future. No, no time travel for me, but it's nice we have the museums. It was rather blunt about the treatment of slaves in London. I stumbled into a class of girls who were listening to a score about "high yellow" slaves. The lady was pretty good with a "slave" accent. The children all listened attentively and asked great questions. I was very impressed with the amount of information they were able to honestly provide. I did find it a bit odd that a pretty much pasty white woman was teaching about being a mixed-race slave. To be honest, those kinds of slaves would look more like me, but I knew all too well that skin color meant nothing. After all, I have a great natural tan, but I only have 3% African in me.

On the 1st floor, the museum displayed information about the modernization of the London docks and the big wars that wiped out half of London. I sat inside a bomb shelter and closed my eyes, trying to picture what it would have been like to be trapped in there hearing all of the guns and bombing happening. The few minutes I sat inside, I felt trapped, and my heart began to race. I shudder at the thought of people sitting in them for days. War is a nasty thing. In my opinion, no one walks away a winner. I wish it weren't so glorified, but I suppose as long as there are power-hungry people, there will always be wars. Some just worse than others.

I found my way to the Exhibit where they talk about building the tunnels and all of the things they found. There were a lot of skeletons. I'm not sure how I would feel, digging into the ground and seeing it was a grave. When we were digging in my backyard and found dead dog pieces, I jumped out of there so fast. I can't imagine how I'd feel if it were a human. Thank goodness there are people out there that don't mind. We learn so much from bones, not an easy job, I know.

I went back into the lobby to figure out my next location deciding it was high time for me to just purchase a map. What a waste of 2.50 pounds, but nonetheless I had one. I sat for about 2.5 hours trying to map out everywhere I had been, and everywhere I will need to go before my trip was over. I had so much to still uncover, but when I went to stand, my leg buckled under me.

The pain was excruciating. I did my best not to cry. What on earth was happening? What had I done to cause it to hurt this badly? I thought back to all the stairs in Paris with my heavy suitcases, and all of the walking in London thus far. "This can't be the end." I thought, but it was hurting so badly. I knew I probably should go to the hospital. When they told me that I tore something in my knee and was suffering from a sprain, I knew the day was over. When I left the hospital, I decided to sit nearby and wait for Michal to get off work. I made my way into the security office inside the Wharf and harassed the two officers in there for about 3.5 hours, trying hard not to fall asleep.

When Michal got off work, Declan picked us up so I could change my shoes and get ready for the pub. I was in such terrible pain, but I didn't want it to spoil my trip. Besides, I was excited to hear the type of music they played in London. I know of some pretty remarkable artists from the UK, so I thought this was going to be good. We each picked a beer, I chose Blue Moon since I wasn't sure what the night would end up like, and I wasn't ready for shots while it was still daylight. I couldn't believe it stayed daylight until 9:30 in London.

We hung out for a while trying to listen to the music, but to be fairly honest, it sounded like the guy was crying and complaining in the mic. I just couldn't vibe with it, but to each their own. When Ishla arrived, we decided to go pub crawling, at least that was the original plan, but hunger took over. We wound up going to SoHo. As we got closer, I got more and more hungry and turning hangry quickly. Declan saw a TGIFriday's, and we popped in for a bite to eat. One of the servers was giving us a hard time because we wanted to sit at a 5 person table and there were only 4, but I insisted on speaking with the manager and of course she understood and permitted us to sit where I wanted. I'm not a fan of pulling the diva card, but sometimes you have to, and with my injury, I needed more space.

We laughed as they brought the food to our table. I being the smallest person, had the largest meal. It was called a Chief Burger. It was a 7 ounce char-grilled burger, piled-high with chicken breast, crispy bacon, Scorpion hot sauce, chilis, jalapenos, cheese, onions, tomatoes, and chili mayo served on a brioche bun with crispy fries and topped off with a scotch bonnet chili. I ate the entire thing. It was so epic and delicious that I actually needed a fourth bun to finish it all. After dinner, we harassed our waitress a little bit. I attempted to get Michal to close the deal with her, but he hadn't. Maybe he wasn't so interested. We also looked at some of the photos Declan had taken. He certainly lived an interesting lifestyle, but it was cool of him to let us in a little. Ishla was extremely quiet. We teased him a bit about getting in the back of a van with a group of strangers. After all, that's how many teen thrillers start. Declan's van could only fit three in the front so Ishla climbed in the back of the van...that had no seat belts.

When we left, we talked about going out to dance somewhere, but Declan gave me the "dad look" and stated that it wouldn't be a good idea - especially with my knee. The truth was, I didn't feel it so much until I stood up. All at once, the pain rushed to it, but I wanted to dance so badly. I'd yet to go dancing, besides that night with Laurent, and well, that didn't really count. Nonetheless, I knew Declan was correct so back into the van we all went, except for Ishla. He said he didn't want to ride in the back again and opted to take an hour-long bus ride back. I can't say I blamed him. We were a group of random strangers he'd just met that evening after all.

Once Declan dropped us off at the flat, Michal and I tried to watch Futurama. I felt the weight of all of my food piling down on top of me, and before I knew it, I was out like a light.

13

Last day in London

I didn't know Michal would be working on a Saturday, so I didn't stress on insuring my alarm was set. The usual extremely loud morning clatter by Michal happened. I awoke wondering what was happening. There was a searing, shooting across my knee, and I was beyond exhausted. I just didn't feel like it today. I had too much on my mind the night before, and passed out while doing some work. We had actually planned to go out that evening, but that clearly wasn't happening with my knee in as bad shape as it was. Michal needed to get going. He wasn't going to work, but he had a meeting with some friends at 9 am. My first thought was, "What kind of friends make you get up at 9 am to hang out?" But then I thought about all the times that I've kidnapped some of my friends and gone hiking to see the sunrise back in California. I got dressed as fast as I could. I wanted a shower, but I totally didn't have the time. I did my best to move quickly, but it just wasn't happening this morning.

Finally, at a quarter to 10 am, Michal told me to just take my time packing, but he had to run. I took the opportunity to go ahead and shower. I knew once I landed in Dublin, I'd hit the ground running. Besides, my skin was acting up. Sometimes my eczema has a mind of its own and flares when it decides to. It's incredibly frustrating to have itchy, dry skin that burns most of the time. I stood in the bathtub with a shower handle. There wasn't a curtain, so I always had problems not getting water all over the place. A part of me wanted to fill the tub up and soak, but with how I was hurting, I was afraid I'd get stuck in the tub and Michal would come home to my drowned, naked body. Instead, I showered and got ready for the day. I repacked my luggage, deciding to leave behind my giant air-mattress and the tiny suitcase. I was sick and tired of luggage fees for something that weighed only 8 lbs.

I was prepping to leave, but Michal's flatmate told me I could just wait a while since she was going for a run. I decided that wasn't a bad idea considering the clouds looked super rough. I sat back on the couch and attempted to rest, but my mind was restless, still very much thinking of the things that were on my mind the day before. What was I really expecting to gain from this adventure? Was I a fool for doing this? How am I ever going to return to the U.S., knowing my heart is in Europe? These thoughts, especially the last, haunted me consistently. Really! How was I planning to go back to California and just fall "in-line" with a routine when my soul craved adventure, challenge, and inspiration...none, which I felt I could find in California.

A bit later, Michal's flatmate walked in completely drenched. I was glad I hadn't attempted to find my way to the airport so early, my poor computer would have been completely destroyed. We sat and chatted for a while then Michal walked in. We couldn't decide on whether we'd go out dancing or stay in. I wish we'd gone dancing even with my bad knee, it would have saved me from hours of defending my faith. Michal simply could not understand why I have faith in Christ, but as I told him, "My relationship with Christ doesn't need to make sense to anyone except for me. As long as my faith doesn't bother (meaning harm) anyone else, its no one's business to understand." People who don't believe, love to attack believers the way believers use to attack non-believers. I think people just need to mind their own business. As long as it's not hurting anyone else...let it be.

14

Dublin

I left Michal's at half-past 1, getting to the airport at a quarter after 4. What a ride. The tram was full of partiers heading home after a drunken night out. A couple of boys sat next to me. They smelled strongly like a variety of booze mixtures. The scent was very familiar, it made me think of everyone back in L.A. I wondered what they were all doing at that moment? Probably out in the nightlife bars, of course. I hadn't really partied at all on this adventure, kind of strange. I mean, I went to that pub with Laurent, but that was really it. I wanted to go to some of the big European discos, but somehow, whenever it became time to go…I was always too tired. I suppose I also didn't feel sexy with all of the random emotions escaping me. I'm usually the "hold it in" type, but this trip has been opening me up. I'm not sure if I like it.

The airline Ryanair was the worst about handling persons in a wheelchair, but the patrons in the airport were even worse! After making it to the airport, I went to find a wheelchair since my legs were throbbing and prevented me from really walking. After checking in, it was half-past 4. It took the airline an hour to get me a chair. Then they made all of us in wheelchairs late for the plane. The people in the airport kept cutting us off as if we were invisible. One guy even bumped my leg with his bag, never excusing himself. I swear people can be so inconsiderate. The elders in the chairs, also were experiencing these issues with people. These budget airlines suck! I often wondered if it would be a better investment to fly with a good-name airline, but a part of me thinks that all airlines suck so it's not worth the money. I understand they have millions of people to deal with a day, but still...take some pride in your work. The lazy people make the excellent workers look bad.

Finally boarding, I started thinking, "Omg! I'm actually going to Dublin!" I wanted so badly to come here for a while, but life always got in the way. Thankfully I am old enough to travel when I want as long as it's financially possible. I began to think about what my relatives were like. I hoped they weren't like my grandmother. I honestly had no clue how I was going to even find them. Dublin couldn't be that big...could it?

It was a shorter flight. Once we landed, I waited for another wheelchair and was pushed to the bus stop. My host, Gui, didn't know there was a marathon going on, so I was not dropped off at the correct location. In fact, I was miles away. It took some time for us to find each other, but eventually we did. Gui was tall with dark hair and a dark beard. I wondered why he looked so Italian, then I remembered that he is Italian and was just in Dublin for work. I had, as some call it, a "blonde moment". We walked for what felt like ages. My weak legs felt like they wanted to fall off, and my tummy was rumbling. I hadn't really eaten in 24 hours, and I could smell pastries, just couldn't see them. We passed a Tesco, which is a European grocery store, and I had a look around. My tummy was not very pleased with what I was seeing, but I needed to get something right away. I grabbed a microwavable meal, a bag of donuts and a bottle of water and we proceeded to Gui's flat.

After a few blocks more, we arrived. It was the only green door on the street, so I guess that was very convenient for me to find later. It was pretty large inside. The house was built upwards rather than wide like American places. There were several bedrooms and two floors with lots of natural sunlight. I loved that you could climb on the roof if you dared...Gui did not. After settling in and eating my donuts and tea, I decided I needed a nap.

Well, the nap turned into a crash, and I slept for 5 hours. I hadn't really slept in over 24 hours, so I certainly needed it. When I woke up, Gui and I went for a food hunt and to see the city center. Dublin's city center was excitingly filled with live music. A few significant buildings to see, tons of shops, even more pubs, and food places. I liked it thus far.

We attempted one of the most famous areas in Dublin, Temples Bar, but it was completely packed. So instead, we went to Gui's favorite pub, Porter House. I had a burger and fries, Gui wasn't very hungry, so he just ate sweet potato fries. I sometimes feel strange when I eat so much, and the guy around eats nothing. I always wonder if I look like a human vacuum to them, but to be honest, I honestly could care less. If I am hungry, I am going to eat...and not rabbit food. We also drank beer. Gui ordered me a type of black beer that was similar to Guinness. It was quite stout and had a strong aftertaste, but I still drank the entire thing.

After food, we walked to meet with some of Gui's friends. By now, my leg was really hurting again, but I didn't want to complain. We walked around for quite a bit then ended up at a hidden party location. It was a regular pub at first glance, then you walk to the back, then down some stairs to reveal another 2 pubs. Over to the right is a corner and another set of stairs that expose you to the outdoor pub area. It was crowded, and I would say that it was absolutely hippie central. The DJ was pretty cool, and the scenery was very "naturalistic." They had a bus they sold pizza out of, and you had to go inside to one of the three pubs for a beer. There was also a flea market going on around the party. The only thing I absolutely hated was all of the cigarettes. I don't know why people think cigarettes make them look cool because they absolutely do not. They make the person and anything they come in contact with stink 100%. They hurt the lungs of others who do not smoke, especially those with lung issues like myself. I didn't want to be there anymore, so after Gui finished his pizza and we finished our beers, we took off back for Gui's flat.

By then, my knee was throbbing again. Gui opted for a taxi. Taxis were so freaking expensive. It made me want to walk everywhere. 12 Euros just to do 6 blocks. We were sitting at a stoplight, and it literally jumped 2 euros. I couldn't believe it. I guess this was normal to Gui, because he didn't blink an eye. We got back to his flat. I started getting very very tired, but was still awake enough, so we decided to watch a movie. We chose "Table 19" since I had been trying to watch it for weeks. We got almost halfway through, and I kept dozing off. By now, it was about midnight, and we were both exhausted. So we just went to bed. I told myself that I would go exploring the next day. I also had a pre-summit review, and I was pretty excited about that.

I climbed into bed. It was quite chilly. I guess a room with no windows and ceramic floors will do that. I grabbed my blankey, swaddling myself. Feeling cozy, I laid there thinking, "I am in Dublin. This is where some of my people came from." I tried to picture what it would have been like to grow up here. I imagined running through the fields and trying to find the castles, eating all the cabbage I wanted and staring up at the stars at night. I quickly drifted off to sleep. My final thought was," What do Irish people eat for breakfast? Meat?". The next moment, I was sound asleep.

15

A whole lotta nada...

Today was a whole lot of absolutely nothing. I woke up semi-early but stayed in bed until noon. What was I going to do with my day? I had a meeting at 5:00 pm, so I didn't want to go super exploring and get all gross. I decided to hang in bed a while and get some work done. I had so many emails that had gone unanswered. People probably thought I fell off of the earth by now.

I took some time to sort my emails and answer my social media. Before I knew it, it was almost 3:00 pm and I hadn't eaten yet. I tried to do some research and see what was around me, I even attempted to go walking, but I didn't really see too many things. I finally caved in and ordered something for delivery. It took ages to get to me, and we had communication issues. Without being able to accept international calls, it made it nearly impossible for the delivery guy to contact me. Over an hour later, my food finally arrived. Unfortunately, it wasn't good except for the onion rings, but I ate it nonetheless. The burger tasted freezer burned and dry as ever. It was worse than a McDonald's burger. That is karma for you. I should have actually gone walking to find the store, but I must admit, I was being rather lazy.

After eating, I opted for a nap, but I decided I wanted to sit on the roof and enjoy some tea. It was mesmerizing, how simple the sky looked, yet it seemed to hold every one of our thoughts, our dreams, our secrets. It was vast, stretching out for infinity over our heads. We are insignificant creatures, being embraced by the forever moving expanse. I sat out there for an hour, embracing the peace that I was feeling, then climbed back in bed and dozed off. When I woke up, it was almost time for my meeting. I was excited until I realized that Gui would not be back from work yet, and I had the only key.

The rep hadn't wanted to meet in my area, so sadly we had to reschedule. I was pretty bummed because I was very much looking forward to discussing my plans with her. I planned to meet with industry reps in each of my locations, but this would be the first of the trip. I wasn't too pleased about that, but what could I do? Instead, we planned for a sunrise-ish shoot and meeting. We were shooting in Dalkey, and I needed to get there as early as possible. I wasn't going to let the photographer or myself down. I agreed to the times, and I started a little prepping. Usually that means packing my suitcases and putting them at the door, but since I was feeling sluggish and engulfed in my work on the computer, I simply discussed details with her and confirmed the addresses.

When Gui arrived, he invited me for dinner, but I was too tired. I think all of my walking in Paris and London had been catching up with me. I decided to stay in and kept working on my computer. I was pretty annoyed with myself for wasting an entire day in Dublin, but I was also so tired that I wouldn't have really enjoyed what I was seeing had I gone out. I took another power nap and waited for Gui's return.

I woke up to an intense pain in my tummy. It felt like I had not eaten for weeks, and everything was now closed. I became very annoyed with myself. Why didn't I go to dinner with everyone? What was I going to eat? Luckily, Gui found a place that was open and brought me home a fish sandwich and some delicious fries. I still had some leftovers from my food earlier, so I combined everything. HORRIBLE IDEA!!! The burger was even worse than the first time I ate it, but I refused to waste food. I sucked up my pride and ate it all. I felt so gross, but I got over it.

I thought about watching a movie with Gui, but he had to get up for work, so he was too tired. Instead, I went out on the roof and just looked up at the sky. The air was crisp and a bit chilly. I wasn't sure if it would rain or not, but I didn't care. It felt good up here. It felt peaceful, and that was most important. I don't know exactly what it is about traveling, but I seem to have been less and less stressed on this trip. Usually, Derek is with me, and he finds a way to screw up the traveling. One day, he booked the wrong flight simply because he hadn't read the information that was presented to him. He had wasted over $350 USD! I was so annoyed that I ended up taking all responsibility when we traveled. I held on to everything from our transport papers, airline tickets, baggage tickets, and passports. I didn't want to ever risk not being able to travel. I also had to take over packing the car and luggage because he'd left luggage sitting at the front door before and it cost a lot to replace all the stuff inside of it… I am still repaying that debt. Derek, overall, just wasn't good with traveling. Thankfully, I didn't have to worry about any of that. This time it was just me. I was in Dublin, on the roof, enjoying the peace.

I started thinking again about everything I had been going through and where I currently was. Life really had dealt me a tough card from birth, yet here I was..in Dublin of all places. I've gone through, and I've overcome what most could never. I think God knew my life would be hard, so he gave me a bit of extra strength. Sometimes I think about quitting, but what else would I do? I was too stubborn to sit on the ground and watch life pass me by. My only option was to keep fighting for what my heart desired, a place where I belonged....even if I had to create that place myself.

16

So early

I set my alarm for 5 am, but it took me until after 6 to actually get up and get going. I ended up having to rush for my shoot because I wasn't exactly sure where the train was nor how to get there. I quickly got dressed and left the house at about 20 after 7. I was pushing my suitcase down the street, and people were staring at me. It was far too early for me to even think about caring.

I wound up at the wrong bus stop, so I popped into a little store. I was so thankful they were open because I also needed to get change for a ticket. I had to ask two different people for directions, thankfully there were a lot of morning runners running around that were kind enough to assist me. I made it to the station with 2 minutes to spare, but the darn ticket machine took those two minutes, and as I ran through the gate, the train was literally pulling off. I felt like the guy in those movies where he gets there too late, and his love is gone forever. Usually, he turns around, and she's standing there ready for him to embrace her, but no, not this time. Not for me. The train was gone, and all I could do was wait 45 minutes for the next one. My photographer was not going to be pleased, but I at least had been keeping communication with her.

An hour later, I arrived in Dalkey. She met me at the train station and walked me through the town. It was quite beautiful. She even showed me where Bono eats lunch, which was pretty cool. Once we got to her flat, I quickly changed into the first dress. We only had a little less than 2 hours to create absolute magic with 3 outfits in 3 different locations, and one took a little time to get to.

We started with the rose-colored dress that came from Puerto Rico. It was long and flowy. It expanded, opening a little at the feet, more like a flowy trumpet gown. The top sat just on the edge of the shoulders, and it was very form-fitting, all made of lace. When I looked at this gown, I immediately thought of traditional Puerto Rico. We climbed on top of some rocks, and the scenery was fantastic. It looked like something out of a fairy tale, and I was the Goddess. We also shot a blue dress I designed. It, too, was long and form-fitting. It had netting panels crawling up the hips in just the right places that made it very sexy, but still seemingly conservative. There was a little dog named "Snow" that kept trying to join in the shoot. He was quite cute, but I was worried about him with my white gown. Katrina said we were going to move locations for it. We had just one more site with the blue dress.

When moved to the second location which was on a fisherman's boat. It didn't smell the greatest, but I didn't care. I knew the photos would be worth the stench. The fisherman helped me into the boat, and I climbed on the front. Then he picked me up and put me on the very top on the front of the boat. There was a little wind, so the boat was rocking a bit. I had to hold my breath and tense up so I wouldn't wobble into the water. We shot at the boat for only a few moments because it was now time for the big white dress. I quickly ran to change. We only had maybe another 15-20 minutes tops to get the right shot and we were totally going to go for it. We hopped into the car with the fisherman. I, of course, was still trying to get in on the wrong side of the car. I walked around to the left, and we stuffed me and the gown down into the car, setting off for location number three.

We parked over on the seaside with a secret bridge that was not underwater because of the tide. Katrina kept saying how much she wanted that shot and she kept apologizing to me that we couldn't get it. I looked down at the dress then yelled, "Fuck it! Let's do it". I got in the water. The first few steps were extremely icy. It was still rather chilly in Dublin, and the water felt like winter waters as if there was tons of ice in it right where I was standing. The iciness sent chills straight through my entire body, but I kept telling myself to just hang in there, that the shot would be totally worth freezing.

I walked along the hidden bridge, submerging my gown in the icy, freezing water. The train kept getting trapped on the rocks, but at the end of the day, we got the shot. The fisherman kept looking at me strangely. I tried not to think about it too much while we were working, but it was tough to stay focused. He seemed so familiar, but I couldn't remember where I'd seen him before, especially since this was my first time in Dalkey. It was later revealed that he knew my gran and was in the photo I'd seen of her. We thanked the fisherman and returned to Katrina's place. Then I made my way back to Gui's place and decided it was time for a rest, but first food!

I quickly warmed up all of my leftovers from the night before and damn near swallowed them whole. I tried making plans to explore. I met up with a kid for an hour. He was determined to hang out, and I decided that I couldn't stay my last night inside. We walked around the river and near town for a bit. He kept trying to get me to go to the city center, but I simply didn't want to. The more I hung out with this kid, the more I realized that I just wanted to go home. He actually told *me* that smoking was good for your body. I nearly lost my head, but I kept my cool and stopped into the nearest grocery. There we decided we should part ways (thank the heavens), and I picked up a bag of donuts. I figured I deserved a reward for dealing with that nonsense.

I was heading back to the flat but was stopped by a lady that saw me when I was pushing my suitcase down the street that morning. She called to me, "Hey, you're the lass dragging the case this morning, aren't ya?" I told her, "Yes." trying to figure out what trouble I've gotten myself into now. She looks at me then appeared taken aback. "Didn't you have black hair this morning? Did you die your hair that quickly?" she questioned. I smiled and attempted to explain to her, but it was just easier to show her. I took off my wig, and her eyes enlarged. "By the Gods. Step in here and let me see how that works ya." I stepped into her house as she took her scarf off. I asked her if she wanted to try on my wig. With great enthusiasm she says, "Oy, yer darn right I do!" putting on my wig. Moments later, her husband walks in. "Darla! What ave ya done to yer head?" he questioned. The look on his face was priceless. I don't even think it occurred to him that a stranger was standing in his living room, he was so preoccupied with what his wife was doing.

She tells him that they're getting her a wig and I walk her through wig 101. It was quite amusing watching her take notes on the subject. "Well, I'll be damned." she says as my lesson came to an end. I told her that she can swap them out per her mood and her husband didn't seem to like that idea so much. "Oy, don't ya go encouraging that. She'll be round her looking like a smurf." Apparently, Mrs. Darla was known for the dramatics. They do a bit of married couple bickering, and I got an idea. I ran back down the street to my things and grab one of my other wigs then ran back to her place.

"Here." I say, handing her the wig, "When it gets tatty, go to this website or call this number. Tell Mark that Anaís sent you. He will take good care of you." I wrote the information down for her, and a huge smile spread across her face. "Great stars. You don't know what you're doing here." I smile back at her, feeling pretty great that I could extend my love of wigs. I tell her that it was no problem. She stood there in the mirror, playing with the wig for a few moments. The entire time the husband stood there quietly staring at his wife. When he finally spoke, he moved closer to her and grabbed her into his arms, saying, "Hey er, let's go out on the town tonight." The tone in which he spoke told me I needed to get out of there and get out of there quickly. I didn't think they'd make it out of the house as I'm sure they were about to get it on. Hair can do wonders for confidence. I know one day my hair will grow back from the chemo, and I won't have to wear the wigs anymore, but I have to admit that I love the convenience of them.

I left the couple and went back to the flat. I pigged out a bit more, then decided it was time for a nap. I tried hard to fall asleep, but it wasn't happening. Gui came home a while later, and we decided to order pizza and watch a movie after I finished packing. Another traveler wanted to meet, but I told him I had to go to the airport, he volunteered to drive me, so I gave in. It took me a while to meet with him, but I finally did a bit after 1 am.

Gerry was a Dublin native. He was tall and slender. To be honest, he looked more German than Irish to me, but then again looks are always deceiving. We drove around for a bit and stopped at a shipyard. There were tons of sailboats. I could see the stars a little, and I started quickly getting sleepy. I felt terrible for the guy because I wasn't really holding a good conversation with him, I was just too exhausted. A little while later, he dropped me off at the airport, it was finally time to explore Italy. I was pretty excited for Milan, being it was pretty top on my list of fashion places to visit.

17

Milano

I arrived in Milan in the climate height of the afternoon. It was completely different weather from my other locations. It was most certainly time to store the big red coat and pull out the booty shorts! Once I arrived, my host met me at the metro station. Daniele was just as I imagined him, though he didn't have a crazy thick Italian accent. He was average height with brown hair and hazel eyes, and he spoke perfectly good English. I don't know why that is always such a shock to me, but it usually is.

We walked about three and a half blocks to his place. He was very kind to assist me with my luggage, especially since it was extremely heavy. We walked into the building and into the lift. Whew! It was really warm out. Such a serious climate difference for sure. We put my things down, and he asked what my plans were. I initially considered going to explore Milan at night, but he pointed out that I hadn't slept in 24 hours, and it was scorching outside. Instead, I opted for a nice nap.

I ran to the café for a panini and went back to get into the bed. Daniele's bed was pretty large, but I hadn't really paid any attention. I pretty much passed out immediately after eating the panini. When I finally woke up, about 4 hours later, I got to work on my computer to see what I'd been missing. It wasn't long after that Daniele walked in. "What do you want to eat?" he asked. Of course, my answer was "Meat!". I really don't think I could live without at least chicken. I guess its mostly because I'm so tiny that I need the extra protein and such...I also enjoy the taste.

While he cooked, Daniele played Green Day's "Welcome to Paradise". We both found it rather amusing since it was the title of my journey, and he said it reminded him of me. Daniele was very goofy, which I liked. I love meeting silly people who are still serious enough to handle their responsibilities. He seemed to be the very person. As he prepped dinner, we caught a stunning sunset. It was absolutely magical. It appeared as if Milan's sky was on fire with startling oranges and reds fused with hints of yellow and lavender colors. It was indeed one of the most magnificent sunsets that I've seen in a long while.

We sat outside to eat dinner with the smell of jasmine filling our noses and the air around us. It was all so lovely and absolutely relaxing, just what I needed considering how busy my days leading up to it had been. I allowed myself to relish in the moment. I was still getting used to feeling such peace in my life. I hadn't had anyone to look after, except for myself now, for 2 weeks. I had hardly been in communication with anyone back in the States. If it wasn't a client, I didn't bother responding much. I was just appreciating this much needed "me-time". I wondered, "Why hadn't I done this sooner?" but I knew the answer to that. I always put everyone and everything else in front of what my heart wanted...not anymore.

After dinner, a familiar feeling filled me. It was time for a snack attack. Daniele agreed to show me a place that would be open. Down the street, around the corner, and through the park, we went. I could smell BBQ. At first, I thought I was just being a fatty, but as we got further on our journey, we passed a random eatery that was full of people and good music. I was correct about the BBQ because it was coming from inside. Daniele told me that you could purchase meat and take it there to grill and have drinks with friends. The temptation to enter the place was so high, but I was not at all dressed for such an occasion. In other words, I was now down to my PJ's and sunglasses. Daniele found it amusing that I wore them at night, but I was so used to always having them on, now without them, most lights hurt my eyes. Even when I'm on stage performing, my eyes are usually closed since glasses aren't often a part of my costume.

We found a 24-hour grocery, and my tummy tried taking over. I started grabbing so many things I thought would taste fantastically. Suddenly I realized that I was only there for two days, and I decided I should only get what I would eat that night. I grabbed a handle of peaches, chips, frozen ravioli, and a tea. I felt kind of silly getting the ravioli since I was now in pasta land, but my tummy didn't care and wanted it anyway.

We got the snacks and headed back to the flat. We decided to watch a movie even though we were both now super full. Literally 15 minutes into the film, we were both passed out. Hours later, Daniele tried to wake me up. That was a task, and then some, for him. I sat up finally, so confused. I couldn't figure out what to do with the bag of chips that was in my hand. "Wanna go to bed?" he asked. All I heard was the word "bed", and I made my way to his room and climbed in without a second thought. I heard him say something about the window, but I grumbled and passed back out.

18

Exploring Milano

I decided to wear the floral dress I wore in Paris. I wanted to feel cute when I strolled through the streets, which also meant I was going to be wearing my heels too. I left Daniele's a bit after noon. I went on a breakfast hunt before my adventure began. The first two places I stopped didn't speak a lick of English, and it was too stressful to try to translate, so I kept looking. Finally, I found a little patisserie and got a treat. It looked so amazing and was large enough for two, so I ran back to Daniele's place to share with him. It was delicious and similar to a pain au chocolat, but I couldn't help but wish it was warm. Nonetheless, I enjoyed every bit of the treat and set back out on my adventure.

The manager at the metro gave me a map of Milan and pointed me in the direction I wanted to go in. When I got off at my stop, I was still quite lost, but decided to just keep walking and see where it would lead me. I walked a good bit and found myself in the middle of the fashion district. All of the top brand names were in this area. I saw so many beautiful things. I had to keep telling myself to keep my hands to myself and not in my wallet. It was very easy to spend all your money with all the stunning dresses I saw.

I approached a massive church. It was beautiful, but the guards wouldn't allow me to enter...even when I pouted. Apparently, you had to purchase your tickets online and prior to arriving. Then you still had to wait in an extremely long line. Instead, I went into the bath bomb store "Lush". The smell was super intense. It almost blasts you before you even get through the door. Joey had brought me one when I was going through my illness once, but I hadn't used it yet. I was waiting for just the right moment. I started to get him something from the store, but had no clue what smells he liked; instead, I only took photos of everything.

After I was done drowning in rich, fragrant scents, I furthered my walk around to the front of the cathedral. I was strolling along, minding my own business, when randomly this guy grabs my hand and fills it with popcorn seeds. I look at him very confused then he whistled. All of a sudden, hundreds of goddamned pigeons flocked to me. I was so freaked out and angry. What was he thinking? I can't stand those birds, they poop on everything. I squealed and tossed the seeds in the air.

After finally getting the birds away from me, the guy had the gall to walk up to me asking for money. I asked him how much and this fool had the nerve to say "20 euros." I laughed. For popcorn seeds you forced into my hand to feed disgusting pigeons...ummm no! He wanted to keep discussing it, but I told him I wasn't even going to give him 5 euros, and he said, "Fine, fine. Bye." What on earth had I walked into? Before I could complete this thought, another guy grabbed my wrist and put on two bracelets. One was for luck, and the other was for love. He too, then asked for money, so I gave him 1 euro since I liked the bracelets. I realized this was a tourist trap, but I was refusing to be a further victim.

I made my way down the street toward the Castello Sforzesco thinking I was free from street hustles, but I was very wrong. A creepy guy dressed in a Victorian-era costume kept flirting and trying to steal a kiss. I wanted more than anything for him to let me go. He was a creepy Italian mime. I gave him 20 cents, and a card, then rushed off only to run into another. He actually asked to come back to my hotel. What were these guys doing? They were so very creepy. I pushed away and didn't stop or let another come anywhere near me.

Finally, away and safe, I crossed the street to the Castello Sforzesco. It was incredible. It too, had guards sitting outside the gates. I walked in and around a bit. It wasn't long before I got lost in the massive park portion. I am always getting lost. You'd think I'd get the map out, but I didn't. I just kept wandering around until I found an exit. Walking around outside was more than a bit of a headache. These guys from, I'm guessing, Ghana just wouldn't stop bothering me. You tell them "No." and they still follow you. You ignore them, and they still follow you. I like persistent guys, but come on. There is being persistent and being a total forcing creep.

I got out of there as soon as I could. I managed to find my way to a random aquarium. I walked inside, and there were so many different fish. I still couldn't believe that I haven't gone to the ones in the States. Inside one of the tanks, was a bunch of "Dories" and puffy fish. My inner child totally escaped. I started squealing "Dory!!!" with the other children. I went outside into the garden, and the excitement furthered. There were coy fish and turtles!! It all certainly entertained me for that hour and a half.

After leaving the aquarium I didn't know what else to do, and my knee was hurting, so I decided to hop on the next bus I saw. What I hadn't planned on was falling asleep on it for 2 hours, but I totally did. I thought I was being spontaneous and seeing where it took me, but all I saw were the insides of my eyelids. Literally, 15 minutes after getting on the bus, I leaned over and crashed out. When I finally woke up, we were passing a café. Go figure. I decided that it was time to get off before I ended up in another country.

I jumped off the bus and headed towards the nearest metro. I was so exhausted that I needed to get home and in bed. I hopped on the underground and headed back to the flat. All of the day's craziness was done, and I could relax...or so I thought.

As I am exiting the Metro tunnel, a guy walks up to me and says, "Hey, have you been waiting long?" I looked at him baffled. "No." I replied, and I continued to walk to the street. The guy followed me saying, "Okay cool. Well, let's walk together." Still totally confused and stunned, I started walking slowly, trying to figure out who this person was. He said, "I have been very anxious to meet you." then starts talking about the types of women he dates and how I am different. Mind you, this guy is clearly in his 40's so not really my type. I still didn't have a clue who he was. Thankfully, Daniele appeared, and I hugged him tightly. I was thrilled to see him. I told the random guy that I had to leave. He didn't like that idea. "Oh, already?" he asked reaching for my hand. I stepped closer to Daniele and told the man that I had to leave. I couldn't understand who or what he was talking about. I really had no clue who he was, and I wasn't interested in sticking around to find out. I grabbed Daniele's arms and turned to walk away.

Daniele asked what happened, and I explained it as best I could. He couldn't stop laughing. This type of stuff I would have never believed if I hadn't been going through it myself. We laughed and talked about my day over dinner. As we discussed my next travel plans, Verona popped into my head since we were talking about Shakespeare. I went into a "fit" realizing that Verona was only an hour or so away. I wanted to go so badly! I tried several things to change my flight, the only other option was to go to bed then get up at 6 to call the train office and see if it was possible. I wasn't happy, but I accepted the plan and went to get ready for bed.

Daniele told me that he never shares his bed with guests, that he usually pulls the bed out of the sofa and I felt so embarrassed. I was in such a daze that when he said the word "bed", I went straight to his bed and passed out. Not just that, but I had taken his normal side of the bed too. I was intruding on all levels, but thankfully, he laughed and said it was okay. After dinner, we got in the bed and decided we'd try to watch the movie again. Less than 20 mins later…we both passed out…again.

19

Milano to Florence

Had a silly morning with Daniele before I left. We woke up early to call the train station to see if they would change my ticket so I could go to Verona. Sadly, we couldn't actually reach anyone. I sucked up my pride and accepted that I could not, at the present time, go to Verona. We attempted to take a nap, but my tummy was not having it. I sprung up screaming, "Bacon and eggs!!" Daniele looked at me like a was a looney, perhaps I was, but I knew exactly what I was craving...which is rather rare.

We got up and decided we'd go on one last food hunt. We stopped at several places, but no one had what we were looking for. There was one last place he had in mind before we would decide to give up and hit the grocery store. We walked in, feeling hopeful as he asked him if they could make a bacon and egg sandwich. The couple laughed and said, "Yes." Hooray!! We walked to take a seat, but something didn't feel quite right. "Daniele, why are they laughing at us?" I asked, looking back at the couple. "I don't think they are. They're just nice." he replied.

Moments later, the wife approached us and spoke to Daniele. I knew it! It wasn't until he translated it for me that I knew they were truly joking with us, but I knew something wasn't right. "They were joking because they thought we were joking." he said. With a solemn look on my face I asked, "So no bacon and eggs?" "No," he said, "but we can run over to the grocery." After a 15-minute grocery run, we grabbed everything we needed to make a yummy sammy and rushed back to his flat. After all, I still wasn't packed. We rushed up the stairs. Daniele opted to cook breakfast for me while I hurried and got ready. Had I known what a disaster it was going to be my first day in Florence, I wouldn't have even bothered.

After a seemingly short train ride, I arrived in Florence. I almost didn't make it since I fell asleep on the train and had woken up just in time to get off. I still hadn't heard back from my host, and that was becoming very annoying. One of the things I absolutely cannot stand is terrible communication.

I got off the train and walked towards the bus stop to check my phone. "Get on bus 23b." my host said. I had a look around and walked up to the bus stop to read the signs. "Hmm, no bus 23b." I thought to myself. I looked around for help. I saw a middle-aged woman, and I attempted to ask her directions. She ignored me. I said it in Italian, and she literally turned her back to me. What the living FUCK?! I went to another woman, and the same thing happened. Was I being punked or were the women shunning me? I had experienced this a little in Milan as well. I chalked it up to them just not wanting to be helpful, but now I was taking it personally. It was 87 degrees Fahrenheit, my suitcase wheels were broken, my backpack was extremely heavy, I was hungry, and ever so thirsty. I didn't have the patience to be dealing with some rude woman. I asked a guy, who looked to be all of 16. "Around the corner and the first stop." he said. I dragged my heavy load over to the stop only for a girl to tell me that it was the stop I had just come from. I decided to stop and ask a guard.

The guard walked me around the street and pointed at the station that I had just come from. Were these people pulling a coach Gail on me? You see I had this English teacher in high school who was a dick to the first years. They'd ask for a building, and he'd direct them across the football field. Funny, but cruel and I felt like this is what they were doing.

Back and forth I went looking for this stop until finally, someone was willing to check it on their GPS. I tried everything to connect to the wifi, but it wasn't working, and my back up phone had died. Thankfully, a girl helped me find the location. I was actually supposed to take 2 buses to bus 53b, and it would drop me off seemingly nearby. It truly would have been great if the host had given me those instructions.

I got on Bus 14 and took it to bus 22 and then to bus 53b. Looking out of the window, Florence was beautiful. Tons of old buildings and a stunning river that ran through the middle of town. After getting on Bus 53b, I asked the driver if it would get me close to the host's address. He said, "Yes, but no. It is still a far walk." Ughhhh, I was already so tired from trying to find the bus earlier! I thanked the driver, and I mentally prepared for the upcoming hike. So far, I was so not pleased with Florence.

Once the bus got close, I tried to get off, but too many people were blocking me, and for some reason, just wouldn't move. The driver dropped me off even further away. I was not happy, but what was I going to do about it? I took a sigh, got off the bus, then headed for number 53.

"47,48,49,12…wait, what the fuck? Where are the 50's?". The numbers were all wonky, and it was not easy at all dragging my broken suitcase. I saw a couple, and they tried to help me find the address, but they too were new to the area. I was feeling extremely discouraged and was tired of being lost, but there was nothing I could do except continue walking around searching for number 53. Unfortunately, it was 2 hours later when I finally found it. I knocked on the door and then rang the bell. "Yes!?" shouts a woman from an open window above. "I'm looking for Palo." I say, still trying to catch my breath. She buzzed open the door, and I walked in.

I wasn't exactly sure where to go because he still hadn't given me any type of exact directions. Moments later, she came down the stairs and handed me the phone. "Hello?" the voice says. It's Palo. "Hello Palo, I am here." I tell him. "Hi Anaís, I am seeing the museum because I thought you were coming earlier." Are you freaking kidding me? After all of that, this kid wasn't even here?! What was I supposed to do? "You can walk around and see Florence if you like." he said not fully understanding that the last thing I wanted to do was more walking. I was more than annoyed that he had been so horrible with communication. Instead of losing my temper, I calmly explained to him what happened and that he didn't give me proper directions. He told me he would be back later and to find the room that was made up for me.

I dragged my pack and suitcase up three flights of stairs and into the bedroom. "Fuckin' hell man!" I exclaimed finally dropping my backpack up, but remembering my laptop was in there so trying to do it seemingly gently. Palo's mother had left for work, and her mate had disappeared. I decided to lay down for a moment, seriously contemplating a nap. Unfortunately for me, my nap was interrupted by my rumbling tummy. I decided to walk around and try to find food.

The foodie God's were smiling upon me because I found a grocery store. I felt like a person who had been trapped in the desert without food and water and had finally found a lake and tree full of berries. I walked around a bit, trying to keep calm. I knew how my tummy behaved in grocery stores, and I couldn't afford an accidental splurge. I found the tea I had tried with Daniele, some donuts and interesting looking pasta (since Palo hadn't had a microwave) then I headed back for the house.

The weather wasn't so bad if I didn't have that heavy pack on. Sure it was almost 90 degrees, but I actually enjoy the summer heat, though I suppose this was Spring for them. I took a look around and realized everything was closing. I had forgotten about "siesta". Siesta is a specific time of day that businesses close and people take a nap. I loved the idea of it so much. I wonder why American's weren't on board with this beautiful idea?

About 20 minutes later, I arrived back at Palo's place. I opened the door to be greeted by him. I did my best to hide my utter frustration since I didn't want to be rude, and Palo looked extremely young. In my opinion, he looked to be around the age of 18 or younger. He had fluffy dark hair and kind of reminded me of Gordo on Lizzie McGuire. With him was another traveler named Hanah. She was a bit taller than I, her face reminded me of the "crazy girlfriend" meme, but she seemed a lot less crazy.

We all sat in the kitchen eating snacks. We each talked a little about our lives and why we were traveling. Everyone is always so interested in hearing how the American feels about what's happening in my country and how I feel about having Trump for a President. I find it both amusing and annoying, but I'm getting used to it. After awhile, Hanah and I went to see if we could find the perfect view for the sunset. Unfortunately, she and Palo talked for too long, so we didn't have much time. We walked around for a bit, then finally found our way to the river. It wasn't near as stunning as the one in Milan, but the scenery was still beautiful.

We started walking back in hopes that we'd catch the grocery store open. On the way, my nose was filled with the smell of grilled meat! I literally followed my nose to some type of festival. There was live music, but most importantly, *food*. Hanah and I walked to the entrance, but we noticed there was a fee to get in. Considering we didn't know if we'd actually enjoy it or not, we decided to not stay and kept heading towards the grocery store. I looked at my phone and told her we needed to hurry if we were going to make it on time. Sadly we did not.

We rushed to the Coop, but it was closing in 9 minutes. We walked in to ask if there was anywhere else to eat food around here, but the people were so rude. They kept saying, "No closed-no closed." I wanted to snap, but I walked towards the manager who also kept saying, "No closed." I was ready to scream, "Shut the fuck up for 2 seconds and listen!" What was it with Italians - at least the ones I was meeting? They just talk and don't listen at all. I loudly spoke over the manager, "If you will just STOP TALKING for a moment. That is NOT what we are asking. We are asking is there a restaurant nearby or another 24-hour grocery?" He said, "Oooh restaurant!! Yes, there is one down the street some. Ok, you leave my store now." Ugh, I swear people make you just want to kick them right in the shins! There was absolutely no reason for him to be such an asshole.

Hanah and I decided to just walk back to the house and see what was there. Palo's mom was making some pasta and offered us some. I was grateful. I went into the kitchen to help, but she told us to sit and rest. I watched as she prepped the food. I'm personally not a fan of left out food, and the eggplant had been left out literally all day in 86 degree heat. I politely declined. I didn't want to come off rude, but I'm a bit funny with my food - especially with cleanliness. I told myself I needed to let it go when I watched her eat a piece of bread off the same floor that we all had been walking on. I told myself, some people are just different. When the pasta was ready, I ate it. I desperately wanted some meat, but Palo was a Vegan, so they didn't keep much meat around.

By now, I was feeling pretty weak and drained and somewhat annoyed with the entire day. I thought about going out, but I decided that I would just rest and figure out something fun to do the next day. I was more than over this day.

20

Wine country

I woke up, still feeling quite annoyed with the world, and took my time to sort my day. All night Palo's cat, who I didn't even know existed, kept trying to get into the room. There was cat hair all over my stuff. I had literally had my fill of cats for the next 50 years. Besides, he never said he had a cat. I'm allergic to them, and I don't like other people's pets. I hadn't got much sleep the night before, so needless to say, I woke up a bit grumpy.

I ate a frittata with everyone. Palo was rushing me to leave, but he still hadn't communicated any of the plans. They, he and Hanah, were going to the city center and I wanted to go to a winery to see some of Florence's history. Palo hadn't told me what time I needed to leave until 20 minutes before he was ready to go. That's the issue with some hosts, you have to leave when they leave, which would generally be okay if it had been communicated prior…but it wasn't.

I informed him that it would be at least an hour and a half before I was ready. I was trying to schedule a trip to the winery, and I had no clue how the bus system ran. Luckily, I met another person that lived in Florence that wanted to go and they had a car. Palo didn't seem too pleased at the idea of waiting, but what else was I going to do? It was 2 pm and scorching heat outside already. Also, once I left, I wouldn't have WiFi. So I had no choice except to wait on the person that was picking me up.

Much to my dismay, he was awful with time. He told me he'd arrive for me at half after 1 pm, but it was already 2:20. I decided to walk to the grocery. I needed to get out of there with the cats, my skin was bothering me so badly. I went to try and find my donuts again, but there weren't any. I was pretty bummed out. Finally, another hour later, Raphael showed up. His reason for being so late was "Italians aren't great with time." A load of crap if you ask me, but I wasn't going to complain too badly. After all, he was driving me to the winery. After stopping at another grocery, and me grabbing some fruit and snacks, we headed off for wine country. We didn't exactly know where we were going, but that was okay to me. We just kept driving and taking photos along the way. We ended up hunting down an old burial grave.

It hadn't occurred to me until we were walking in the woods, how badly this could be if it ended wrongly. We laughed about two strangers taking each other on a random adventure and how these were the things scary movies were made of. Nonetheless, we continued on. We got pretty lost, but that was the fun of it. We stumbled upon an abandoned house - old style Italy. I attempted to explore it, but one door was boarded up and locked, and the other entrance was blocked by a lot of tall grass and weeds. Wild snakes liked to hang in tall grass, weeds, and abandoned buildings. so needless to say, we opted to not enter the home. Instead, we explored the surrounding grounds and talked about what I would do to the property if I owned it.

I imagined running a home for those who have no one, and on the land, we'd have a massive garden to make our own olive oil and wine. I'd have a couple of horses for myself and the visitors to use, and I would have a massive kitchen and grill. Guests could visit and work on the land for room and food, and I would work with a local butcher on discount for meats by sending him business. I'd use my excellent networking skills to get the word out about my little place, and I would do my best to help those who would try to help themselves. It would be quite amazing. It's really what I want. When I am incredibly wealthy, I plan to open a place just like that. I hate the idea that there are people who have no one, but they're trying their hardest to survive. I really want to be able to help them.

We drove into Sienna, then made a turn around to see if we could catch the sunset. We stopped in a little town for some food, and it was wild. After chasing down the sunset, we climbed up a little hill to find a crowd of people. They were standing outside of the butcher shop that was giving out free wine and little snackies while we all waited for dinner. I was getting used to the red wine. We were, after all, in the Chianti Winery district. We decided to leave after looking at the menu. I wasn't too fond of the idea of eating the mouth of a cow.

We drove around for a while longer, trying to find places that were still open. We walked into a little eatery that looked pretty good, but I about lost my mind when a guy reached into the brownie samples with bare hands. I was trying so hard not to be a germaphobe, but it was challenging. That wasn't the hardest part. When looking at the menu, I noticed the pasta was 8 euros, but it only came by itself - then the meat was 12 euros and up. It might've come with a garnish of spinach or something. The sides were another 8 euros. My head literally spun. What on earth was I looking at? Why wasn't there a chicken and pasta dish together?! My brain just could not comprehend what I was witnessing. The place actually wanted me to pay 18 euros for 2 pieces of chicken by themselves! I was so beyond confused. Raphael laughed and explained that is just how Italians eat and they usually don't eat pasta after 5pm. WHAT?!?!?!?! What kind of person lives like this? The "fat foodie" in me was having a fit.

We agreed upon ordering both the chicken and the pasta to satisfy my cravings. I was still obsessing over the way they served food and ate in Italy when the waiter brought over some brown wine. I looked at it curiously then looked at Raphael. He explained it was strictly a dessert wine. I decided to pull an "Anaís" and tell him to share it with me. He didn't know that meant he was taking most of the glass and I'd have a super tiny sip. I wasn't really a fan of it. It tasted like caramel mixed with chardonnay. I decided to try it with a bite of chocolate cake. Goodness, my mind quickly changed. It was indeed a dessert wine!

After leaving the eatery, we headed back to Florence. The sky was so incredibly dark that I insisted we pulled over and have a look at the stars. I was so amazed, though. I guess I've always been amazed by the stars. To understand these fantastic balls of fire all surrounding us, just blew my mind. This is one of the reasons I've always loved the countryside. It was so peaceful...exactly what I needed to help me continue on my journey.

We got back in his car and headed back to Florence. It wasn't long before I dozed off. When we arrived in the city center, I woke up a bit groggy. Raphael wanted to walk through the city center and then to a pub - but I totally wasn't feeling up to it at all. My knee was hurting badly, I was exhausted, I had a rather long day the next day, and I still wasn't packed yet. I hadn't genuinely anticipated staying out so late. Of course I went along, the guy did spend the entire day on the most random adventure with me and did all the driving. We walked to the city center and saw all of the cool statues, including the famous David statue. It was magnificent. Such art and great history. It made me excited to know that Roma was next on my list.

Raphael took me to his favorite pub. I felt terrible for it, but I had to tell him that I did not want to go in. I was just too exhausted for it. I knew if we went in, we would have a drink or two to get me perky again and then more shots would follow that. After long, it would be 5 am, and I would be too tired to get up and pack on time. I couldn't risk not getting to the station on time considering I didn't exactly know my way back and it was pretty far from Palo's house. We walked back to the car, and he took me back to the house. I was more than ready for bed. I washed my makeup off, and as soon as my head touched the pillow, I was out.

21

The Road to Roma

No adventure is complete without headaches, and my adventure is only but half over. I woke up extremely frustrated. I hadn't slept much before it was time to pack my case and go. I quickly gathered my things, said goodbye to Palo, and headed towards the bus stop. I was more than ready to leave, though I did wish I had more time to explore Florence. It was quite an exciting place. After an hour or so, I finally arrived at the bus terminal. Up four heaps of stairs, I struggled to drag my pack. I was beyond exhausted. It was 7 in the morning and already sweltering hot. I sat in the waiting area listening to the people, trying to ignore my hunger pains.

Beside me was a family, and the eldest of the children was not in the best of moods. I listened as the mother attempted to discuss the child's behavior, but you could tell he was frustrated. The mother calmly explained why she was disappointed with the child and left him to be. A while later, the child of his own free will, walked over to the mother and apologized. He explained that he was just flustered and his temper got the best of him; then he apologized for disrespecting her position. The mother further explained why it was not acceptable when he behaved that way, and they together discussed better ways for him to handle his frustrations. I was so beyond proud of the mother that I pulled her aside and thanked her for showing not only love and discipline to her children, but respect as well. I believe when you show your children how to be respectful, they will fully understand and in turn, follow that behavior pattern. Too many people think just hitting a child will get the job done. There is a reason why our society is utterly failing, and that is the poor communication across the board. Maybe one day the world will get it, but I was pleased that at least one set of parents did.

A while later, it was time for me to get on my train to Roma. I pulled out my ticket, and I went to the boarding platform. When the train arrived, I attempted to board, but the manager was a complete jerk to me. There was something wrong with my ticket. Instead of him respectfully telling me this and escorting me to speak with a supervisor, the rude, miscreant of a man starts yelling at me and telling me how I'm holding up the train. My temper was very furiously rising. I couldn't understand why this man was treating me this way. By then, I was more than fed up with the rudeness. I was boiling hot. I had hardly any sleep, got lost, my packs were extremely heavy, AND I hadn't eaten at all! I'd been sitting at the station for 2 hours after it took an hour to get there...so I didn't have any more room for nonsense.

The guy started screaming, "I will call the police." So I told him, "FINE DO IT!" I showed him the email of my ticket, the printed paper, and I told him they must have made a mistake. He proceeded to yell at me again and tell me, "You are crazy!

This ticket is no good!" Now I'm more than furious. It didn't help that he started laughing and speaking Italian to someone. It only pissed me off more. Finally, the police came. I showed them my information and told them that I needed some help. They told me they would take me to a supervisor and not to worry. The jerk tried to touch my bag, and I yelled at him "NO! You don't touch! I'm done dealing with you!" and I went to find the supervisor.

I was raging so badly. I got to the counter extremely frustrated and out of breath from pushing my pack. I apologized in advance to the lady, so she didn't feel like I was taking my mood out on her. I still couldn't believe how horrible the people in Florence had been. Perhaps they needed to drink some of that fantastic wine and chill out. I wanted to raise full-on hell, but I needed to get to Roma ASAP. So, instead of losing it, I tamed my temper and explained the situation. I pulled out every bit of evidence that I had. I even pulled my laptop out and showed her the screenshots of my confirmations.

I called my host, Salvatore, to tell him what was happening. He told me to breathe and that it was going to be okay. He was going to try to call the lady and help explain. I handed the lady my passport again, and she promptly got on the phone, figured out the issue, and fixed it for me. Not only did she fix the problem, but she also upgraded me to first class, and apologized for the confusion. She even put me on the very next route to Roma. I was thrilled to see someone who had respect and honor. I always appreciate excellent service. An hour later, I finally boarded the train to Roma. The seats were a lot more comfortable than the other train, but I suppose that's the benefit of a 300 euro train ticket! I plugged in my phone, snuggled into my seat, and I closed my eyes. Before I knew it, I was drifting off to sleep thinking, "Damn. I should have gone to Verona."

A few hours later, the train arrived in Roma. Feeling a bit better than I had earlier, I gathered my things and deboarded the train. I looked around, not quite sure exactly where I was. I asked a nearby guy for directions. Apparently, he thought that was code for, "Grab my bags and carry them." I immediately started feeling uneasy again. Why did this dude just grab my bags? What did he expect from me? I decided to permit him to carry it, not that he was really taking no for an answer anyway. I kept an open, ready hand hovering my case as we wandered through the tunnels of the station. Finally, we got to a very extensive set of stairs. The guy, who had been talking on the phone the entire time, grabbed my case and carried it up the stairs. I started getting a weird feeling, and I kept trying to thank him and walk away, but he took it all the way to the taxi stand.

When we reached the taxi stand, the guy kept asking me ,"All good?" I told him yes several times that someone was picking me up, but he remained. I spoke with a fellow traveler who said he was probably trying to passively force me to give him money…that was not happening. No one told him to grab my bags, and I kept trying to take them back. So now he was going to deal with the word "No." I decided to not even say a word to him. Instead, I stood there looking at my phone until he finally said, "No worries." and walked away. I was relieved when he finally did. The only issue was a stinky smoker that walked up and kept blowing smoke in my face.

Where was Salvatore? He told me to wait at the station for him since it would be complicated to get to his place. I was more than happy to wait because I was tired of getting lost, and I was utterly exhausted. When he arrived, we popped into a local store. I desperately needed a drink. I felt like the sun was making up for all that rain I got in London. It was hot as Satan's balls, but the worst was yet to come.

Salvatore was about average height with dark hair. He wore glasses and appeared to be closer to my age, yet somehow older. I was intrigued. When we arrived at his house, I noticed that it was quite modern. The first thing that caught my eye was his baby grand piano. The house was spotless, which I thoroughly appreciated. He showed me the room that I'd be staying in for the next few days and we went to sit on the patio. I closed my eyes and took a deep breath. It still hadn't hit me that I was in Europe. I'd been so busy in my head that I hadn't truly stopped to take it all in.

I decided to go on an adventure through the city. Salvatore took me on a ride on his Vespa. I felt a little like Lizzie McGuire. He showed me some sites that would be difficult for me to walk to. We went to see the top of Rome, and it was absolutely stunning! Salvatore dropped me off in the Piazza Navona, and I began my Roman adventure. There was something simply amazing and alluring about the architecture and the history in Roma. One of the most brutal places on earth was also one of the most beautiful.

I first got my gelato, and of course, it was mango. Daniele laughed at me because I refused to eat any until I got to Roma. It was quite expensive for ice cream, but I didn't care. I was happy to try it. As I was walking down the street trying to enjoy my Mango Gelato, I was in awe of the city. Moments later, a guy walked up and started talking to me. I understood more Italian than I could respond to, so I asked him "English please" still trying to figure out why he is clearly interrupting my gelato moment. The fool puts his arm around me and says, "You so sexy. I sexy too. We make good sex". I pushed him off and said, "No." He said, "Okay, okay." Then he tried to lick my face. I was so grossed out. Was he serious? I punched him, and a lady laughed at him. I suppose his ego was bruised because he finally walked off.

Trying to shake off the grotesqueness of the previous guy, I wandered around again. In typical Anaís form, I got lost. I looked at my phone's clock. Seeing that it was now 5:00 pm and I only had a little while longer before needing to meet up with Salvatore. A man then walked up and begins talking in Italian to me. I thought, "Ugh, here we go again." I understood him a little and told him there was a party down the street. He asked me where I was going, and I told him I was looking for "old Roma". The man smiled and said that it was getting late, but to follow him. He guided me to the "Fontana di Trevi". It was much smaller than I thought it would be, but fantastic nonetheless. I threw in a coin and sent my wishes to the wind. I smiled, thinking of the Lizzie McGuire movie again. I can be such a girly-girl sometimes.

I shook the thoughts out of my head and re-greeted the man. We walked and discussed Italy and all its glory. I wasn't really sure where we were going, but I was enjoying the conversation. As it turned out, the guy is a great Italian designer. I could feel my business mode approaching. Before I knew it, we arrived at his atelier that also served as his boutique. I was amazed at his creations. I couldn't believe that I was in the atelier of Augusto Crisafulli and had not recognized him! He showed me where he does the work. The shop appeared small from the outside, but it was massive.

When he opened the door to reveal a set of stairs, I started feeling nervous. There was no one there except us after all. I took a breath, and I proceeded down the stairs. When he showed me the newest line designs, I had to keep my composure. Augusto had me try on several different pieces, even his top-secret one! I was so excited, but suddenly that excitement turned to worry. When he went back upstairs to answer the phone, I took the coat off, put it back on the hanger and tried my phone. "No, Wi-Fi." I wasn't feeling so great at that moment. My instincts started getting concerned. I was in the lower level of a shop that I didn't know the address to. I had no Wi-Fi, and I was with a complete stranger that seemed to like to hug me a lot.

I didn't like the odds that were against me. I've seen this play out in too many movies. It goes badly for the girl. I showed him where I put his coat, and I suggested that we go back upstairs. He conceded. There we talked more about his line, and he had me try on what became my favorite piece of all. The leather was so thick, yet it wasn't too heavy. His designs gripped my every curve. I checked the time and knew it was time for me to leave to meet Salvatore, but not before leaving him my business card. I was honored that he invited me to come back the next day. I was over the moon! I couldn't believe what had just happened. Sure I felt a little uncomfortable being the only two people there, but thankfully I kept my wits about me and was sure to put myself into a favorable position to defend myself IF he turned out to be creepy. Fortunately, that wasn't necessary.

I ran around to find the nearest Metro, and I went to head back to Salvatore's place. My excitement was quickly intruded by my hunger. It was about 8:00 pm (20:00) and I still had 8 stops to go before our meeting spot. I also needed Wi-Fi since my hotspot had completely died on me. I exited the Metro and had a look around. Roma didn't have much free Wi-Fi. Actually, Italy didn't have much free Wi-Fi. Ahead of me, I saw a little shop called "Sicila". I knew some places were a bit funny about sharing their Wi-Fi with non-customers so before asking for the passcode, I took a look around to see if there was something that I would like to eat there. After pondering for a while, and looking for something that would satisfy my hunger and not break the bank, I settled on a little thing that was basically a fried rice ball with meat and veggies in the middle. Holy cow it was delicious! It was like one of the most perfect things I had ever tried. How convenient and simple was this little rice ball! I told myself that I would certainly be making it if I went back to the States.

Moments later, Salvatore appeared, and I hopped on the back of his Vespa. When we got back to the house, Salvatore went back out to get wine while I showered. I did my regular shower routine - which basically meant giving a performance of a lifetime to the showerhead. When I stepped out of the shower, I screamed because I didn't know Salvatore was back. That also meant he heard my shower singing, so I was a tad bit embarrassed.

We laughed about it as he prepared dinner for us. I couldn't help but feel the urge to play his piano. I sat at the keys, and he taught me what each foot peddle was for as I attempted to play "Fur Elise." It was so different playing on these keys verses my keyboard. The sound quality was much better too. I told myself that I would purchase one...one day.

Salvatore and I sat outside to eat. It was refreshingly quiet. We discussed my next day's plans over pasta. There was so much more I wanted to see. Roma had such an interesting past.

I especially wanted to see "Old Roma". I love mythology, and Roma being one of the great places for it, certainly intrigued me to see the old buildings and everything. It was going to be tough to do this on a budget, but I'd find a way. I knew I had to be a bit tight, because I needed to get through several days of Barcelona and I only had 100 Euro left. After dinner we discussed watching a movie, but I knew that I had quite an early day arriving shortly, so I retired to bed. I was determined to see all of my sights tomorrow…or at least as many as possible, and I was going to look fabulous while doing it!

22

Beware of the strays

I woke up today feeling excited. I still couldn't believe I was in Roma! I reminded myself that I only had 1 full day to adventure so naturally, I pulled up all the locations from the "Lizzie McGuire" movie and made plans to visit all of those. I pulled out one of my favorite sundresses, packed my flats, and put on my heels. Salvatore sadly, had to work, but he still managed to show me around a little before he took off.

He first took me to a spot to see the best view of Roma. Of course, my nose had led me to a nearby cart, and I purchased the largest donut I'd ever seen. We hopped back onto his Vespa, and the music from Lizzie McGuire began to play in my head again. It was such an incredible feeling. I was honored to be able to be physically there and see everything that I had dreamed of. At that moment, I decided to go back to the Trevi Fountain and really enjoy it. After all, "when in Rome".

As I made my way back towards the Trevi Fountain, I passed a restaurant. It smelled wonderful, but I was on a mission. The bag I packed my heels and everything in was simply my bikini bag, and it was cutting into my skin. I knew the best thing to do was to purchase a little black backpack to carry everything in. As I was looking for a tourist store, two guys appeared. They were trying to talk me into coming into the restaurant. I smiled and told them I had to keep walking. One of them was very tall, goofy spirited and quite handsome. The other was shorter, not as handsome, but had interesting eyes. He told me his name, but almost as soon as he told me, it slipped away from my memory. I felt bad, but didn't want to keep asking so in my head, I called him "Peter".

Peter asked if he could walk with me. I was reluctant, but I was also in a very great mood, so I said, "Yes, you may." It didn't take long to figure out that he spoke very little English and I spoke very little Italian so conversing was going to be tough, but interesting. We walked on as he told me a little of his life. When we reached the Trevi Fountain, I decided to make another wish. A wish for a crazy Roman adventure…I really should have been careful with what I wished for.

I told him that I was going to go see Old Roma, and he said, "Okay." I assumed that he would walk away since I was walking very far, but he walked closely by my side the whole way there. I was just in awe, seeing all the old ruins. They were painfully beautiful. Whenever I tried to get closer, Peter would cling to my hips. I noticed Peter was a bit handsy. I didn't make too much of a fuss since it seemed like he only wanted to hold my hand, but it was quite annoying. He took me around all of "Old Roma", and my heart lurched when I caught sight of the coliseum. I walked all the way to it quickly. The closer we got, the more excited I got. I was still in shock that I was actually there. The place where so many gladiators braved a fierce fight to the death. A bit barbaric…sure…but still very incredible.

After we left the coliseum, I was feeling a bit tired. It was extremely hot, and my sugar was very low. I needed to get back towards the general area, just in case something went wrong. We saw a trolley. Peter looked at me with a sneaky grin, grabbed my hand, and said, "Come on, hurry!" We hopped aboard the trolley. "Are we supposed to have a ticket?" I asked. An elderly lady smiled and replied, "Not if you get off before they do a headcount." I could tell she was a sneaky old fox. I admired her free spirit. Apparently, she too had simply hopped onto the trolley without a second thought...or a ticket. We jumped off once we got back closer to Old Roma and walked back towards the Fountain Di Trevi. I remembered that I was invited back to the designer's studio. I looked at Peter, wondering when he was going to walk away, but he grabbed my hand and kept walking with me. If I were honest with myself, I was a little annoyed by him. He kept trying to get me to kiss him on the cheek or hug him. The word "No" seemed to miss his ears, so I had to just push his face away and wag my finger at him.

Upon reaching the designer's studio, I noticed that it was quite full. I felt surprisingly uncomfortable, so I said "hello" and told him that I would be in contact another time. It's strange, sometimes I revel in walking into a crowded room and other times, I shudder at the thought...this was undoubtedly one of those times. As we walked away, I decided I really wanted something to eat. After walking for what felt like another 30 mins, we stopped in a little eatery and looked at the menu. I was so disappointed that there wasn't anything with meat in it on the list. My mood quickly went south, and Peter didn't seem to notice. His clinginess went to stage three. I placed my hand on the table, and he kept rubbing it. Getting annoyed, I removed my hand. He took that as a sign to touch my arm. He kept saying, "After a while, we go back to your place and rest?" Once again, the word "No" seemed to go right over his head. He took notice that my mood had shifted and on beat, he had potatoes and bacon brought to the table. "This slick boy. How did he know?" I thought to myself, trying to relax a little. The truth is, the vibe I was getting from him was getting more and more strange.

He decided that we should leave and go to the place he manages to eat. I conceded and followed him, after all, what else was there to do. I started thinking to myself, "Maybe I'm not giving him enough credit, and I'm just grumpy from my sugar being so low." We reached the restaurant where I'd met him, and he picked out a table for us then walked away. I took a look around. To the left, there were live lobsters and fish in a tank that you could just choose for your meal, and to the right, a woman was making noodles from scratch. Feeling a bit more at ease and genuinely considering that my mood was an overreaction, I leaned back in my chair and tried to relax a bit. When Peter returned, he brought a bottle of wine and told the chef to make me chicken alfredo with spinach. When the meal arrived, I was anxious to try it. It was a very large serving, which was no problem for me, but apparently a shock to Peter. I suppose he was not used to such a tiny woman with such a large appetite...then again, most people aren't.

After I finished eating, he gave me a grand tour and introduced me to the staff. I felt very welcomed, and began to relax. It was all exhilarating to take it in, and everyone was full of smiles. Moments later, Peter escorted me out of the restaurant and towards the Metro to go back home. We saw a dress in the window of a shop that was so beautiful that he insisted that

I tried it on. Unfortunately, their small was still a little large on me, but he insisted that the manager sought out an extra small. She did, and it fit perfectly.

Peter didn't take his eyes off me as I twirled around. I couldn't stop smiling. "Get it." he urged. Suddenly a thump hit my gut. "What am I doing?" I thought, "I shouldn't be out shopping, I still have more days on this trip." Immediately I went back into the dressing room and took off the beautiful dress. I couldn't let myself get caught up shopping in Italy. It would be far too easy to lose track and come up short in Barcelona. I felt a strange chill as I was dressing again. I turned around and yelled, "NO, SIR!" Peter was attempting to sneak a peek into the dressing room at me.

Almost instantly, the eerie feeling I initially had about him in the beginning, had returned. Peter could tell I was angry. He apologized and said, "It was an accident." but I knew he knew what he was doing - and I knew he knew better. I handed the sales attendant the dress and attempted to walk out of the store. He grabbed my hand, and sorrowfully said, "I am sorry." He then decided he was going to purchase the dress for me. "You look so beautiful." he said, "You must have it." I told him that it was okay, I didn't need the dress, but he insisted. I decided to give in and just leave the dress with him when I left rather than create a scene. I thanked him and the sales attendant, stuffed the dress in my backpack, and made my way to the Metro. Thankfully, Salvatore had messaged me to tell me he was headed to meet me, so I didn't have to walk home.

As I attempted to say goodbye to Peter, once again the word "No" escaped his brain. "You can wear the dress to meet my Mother." he said. I told him, "No. I am not meeting your mother. I want to go home. I have to leave now." "But I will marry you. I will come with you home." What??? Marry him?! Okay, this guy had completely lost it. I told him, "You can't come with me. I need to go." He refused to listen and followed me onto the Metro.

My heart began to race. Is this how people are kidnapped? If so, I was not about to be another victim. I knew I needed to think quickly, and I knew it would take more than just myself to get me away from this guy. I considered that most of the people around me probably only spoke Italian and my Italian was awful, so I typed into my Google translator: "Please help me. This guy is a creep and won't accept when I say 'no'. Please don't let him follow me." and I angled my phone at a couple that looked nice enough. The female immediately picked up my message and greeted me warmly as if we'd known each other for years. She whispered, "We are getting off at the next stop. You can come with us." and she informed her guy about what was happening. By now, my hands were starting to shake. Peter kept trying to grab my waist, but I managed to shimmy him off. Had this been in the U.S., I would have simply put him in an armbar and added pressure to his points, but since I was visiting another country and was not entirely sure on how they handled anything appearing like violence, I decided it was best if I didn't make a scene.

As we all deboarded the train, I saw a military personnel. I had never been so happy to see a person in uniform trotting around with a rifle in my life. I quickly ran up the stairs and handed the officer my phone. He read it and pushed me aside, telling me to "Go. You are safe now." I saw him pull Peter aside, and several officers questioned him. I thanked the girl and her guy and ran back to the train. Thankfully, another was just 3 minutes away, and I jumped on as fast as possible.

After reaching my stop, I got off, ran up the stairs to the café with the rice balls I liked, and messaged Salvatore. It didn't take him long to get me. When he reached me, I gave him a huge hug that he probably was not expecting. This is the second time a random guy in Italy has tried to follow me home. The notion was crazy, but I put it out of my mind while I rode on the back of Salvatore's Vespa, trying to keep my skirt from flashing everyone we passed by.

Tonight was my night to cook dinner for Salvatore. I truly enjoy cooking for others even though the way we cook our food was very different, and I didn't have all of my usual spices. Nonetheless, I made do with what we could find and did my best to create a sauce out of it. It didn't turn out so bad, though I had a couple of glasses of wine while recapping my day to Salvatore so I wouldn't have been able to tell much difference.

He sat and patiently listened, smoking his cigarettes. I wish he didn't, but who was I to tell him otherwise. He asked me if I wanted to go see Roma at night. The idea sounded magical, but I knew he and I both needed to be up extremely early the next morning. He for work and me for my departure to Barcelona. I sadly declined and prepared myself for bed. Salvatore was a fascinating man, and I certainly wanted to know more about him. Unfortunately, time was against me as I was to leave in just a few hours for the next part of my journey. I fell asleep thinking of what Barcelona was going to be like. The song "Strut" by the Cheetah Girls, played in my mind as I drifted off. I was ready for the Barcelona heat!

23

Barcelona

I woke up this morning wondering how on earth I was going to get myself and my things the 2 miles to the Metro Station. Thankfully, Salvatore was willing to drop me off. I stopped in to grab another rice ball at the little corner shop, pulled out all my travel info, and entered the Metro. I'll admit, I was starting to feel the sadness of my return to the States, but "Strut" kept playing in my head, so I was very much looking forward to Barcelona.

I boarded the Metro, then got to the airport where I had a 6 hour wait. It sucked because there was no one to really chat with, and my Wi-Fi was out. What else could I do but sit there? So I did...sit there. But I sat there going over the previous parts of my adventure. It still hadn't quite hit me that I was traveling all over Europe on my own. I mean, OF COURSE I'd realized it, but it hadn't truly settled into my brain. For once, I was enjoying life as it was happening.

Once I boarded my flight, I snuggled into my seat and decided to close my eyes for a while. It didn't last. There was a guy who kept hacking all over everyone. I was so frustrated!

I never understood why sick people get on planes. I feel like they have zero regards for another person's health. I wanted to stand up and cough right in his face, but I wasn't sure if that would get me kicked off the plane…so I opted to simply wrap my head in my blanket, attempting to deflect any possible germs.

The flight itself wasn't so bad. The landing was a bit rough, but I've experienced worse. I got off following the crowd then realized we were all going the wrong way in the empty airport. Finally turning around and finding our luggage, we all headed for security. Much to my disappointment, you don't get a stamp when you fly from Roma to Barcelona. I literally walked in circles for 40 minutes, trying to find someone to give my passport a stamp. I suppose I was just being a bit of a brat and should have been happy I didn't have to stand in the immigration line; however, I really love getting my stamps.

After finally giving up on the passport stamp, I attempted to exchange my money. I felt like the guy was totally ripping me off, so I argued with him for about 20 minutes. He was trying to make me give him 2 extra euros for every pound or dollar he exchanged. I told the guy he was an ass and I put my money back into my pocket deciding that I would sort it later.

Since I was still waiting on my host to find me and I didn't have anything else to do, I decided to wander around. And the "bad-idea-of-the-year" award goes to… ME. I found myself surrounded by airport security guards and their guns. I saw a sign on a wall, and I wanted a closer look. Apparently, it was a restricted area, and I really shouldn't have been over there. The officers grilled me for a few moments, then started laughing. I supposed I did look rather terrified and silly.

As soon as they let me go, I bolted out the door and went to find my host. He ended up having to come inside the airport to find me. We loaded up his car, and my appetite hit me full on. You would have thought that I hadn't eaten in weeks. The issue now was that it was well after 11:00 pm, meaning pretty much everything was closed. My host took me to the beach markets, and I found a burger joint called "Burger Bus". My word, they were absolutely fabulous. They didn't give me any issues about my complicated order (soft fries, no salt). The food was fresh and fast. As they were cooking my food, I took a moment to "examine" my host. He was different than the others. He was shorter, dark hair and had an interesting vibe about him. I wasn't really sure what it was, but I decided to keep my guard up...just in case. I grabbed my food and stepped outside.

Barcelona was very much LIVE. Hookah bars and people everywhere. It surprised me because it wasn't a weekend, but I remembered the big music festival "Prima" was in town. I wished that I'd gotten tickets for it, but it was best that I didn't. I needed to save as much as possible. Gusto, my host, showed me around to all the best night clubs and the beach. I was pleased to know I would be so close to the beach. We drove near his home and parked, then walked several blocks to his home. I was staying in his in-home studio. I was feeling a bit odd, but I decided to just go with it. When we finally approached his house, I dropped a pin onto my maps and sent it to a friend...just in case.

We walked up a flight of stairs and into a tiny one bedroom flat. Gusto apparently slept on the couch and used his room as a studio. It was a typical male's flat - certainly missing a woman touch and not the cleanest, but who was I to judge? We blew up the air mattress, and I sorted my things, ensuring that I would be able to access the Wi-Fi. I attempted to sleep, but I couldn't. I laid there feeling a little uneasy. Gusto was a photographer who was trading a shoot for hosting me. It's pretty normal to do in my industry, but I still felt a bit uneasy. Gusto also was a smoker, and I wasn't breathing the best. I tried to close my eyes and listen to Barcelona, but the mosquitoes were eating me alive. I had no choice except to close the door and listen to some music.

I had no clue what I wanted to do the next day, just that I wanted to go exploring. Once again, "Strut" played in my head. I smiled, realizing that I was in freaking BARCELONA! I decided that I would use this time to attempt to find my family in Alicante, which was much more south. Clearly, I wouldn't be able to go there, but I had word that they often had relatives in Barcelona and that is where I would start…after I got food, of course.

It's crazy, I know that I knew what I wanted, but there was always a part of me that wondered if I'd ever actually be able to travel. But here I was… alive and well in Barcelona. I decided that I would make the absolute best of this, and it would be incredible. Little did I know what was coming over the next couple of days…

24

descubran mi Barcelona

I woke up having sunk into the middle of the air mattress. I suspected there was a big hole because my body was literally laying on the floor. Feeling annoyed, I sat up and took a look around. Remembering that I was in Barcelona, I smiled to myself deciding to get dressed. But where was the bathroom? I crept out of the studio and looked around at the strange environment. The size of the place wasn't at all the issue. After all, it was just him. It was more of how unclean he kept it and all the food that laid out instead of in the fridge. I had to remind myself that many single guys and girls don't have the best housekeeping habits. I walked into the bathroom and all my domesticated instincts perched. "Ew, ew, ew." I thought. How does one live like this? I couldn't imagine, but then I remembered my grandfather's house in Chicago and how awful it was. I suppose the "neat freak" in me was just bugging out. I started feeling guilty for my thoughts, so I shook them out of my mind. I rinsed out the shower and began my morning routine. It was a little tricky with the small amount of space, but not impossible. I suppose that was the American in me, I'd become accustomed to a bit more space. Truth be told, I didn't have my own bathroom and room until I was an adult. I've always shared. I believe I spoiled myself with my master suite.

After getting dressed, "Strut" popped in my head, so I jammed out to it. I started feeling really great about this adventure. I was looking forward to seeing what Barcelona had to offer me, but first...FOOD. When I stepped out, I decided to take photos of the apartment and a few buildings around it so I could find it again. I wasn't exactly sure of where I was going, but off I went. Making a right then 2 lefts, I realized that I was walking in a circle. I could smell the beach, so I followed the scent. Unfortunately, that scent was distracted by fries, and I wandered into a little shop to purchase $10 worth of fries. I'm sure the people thought that I was absolutely crazy, but I was in a blissful state. I don't know what it is about french fries, but they're holy potatoes.

I kept walking around, passing many little shops. In front of one of them was a group of people chatting. I loved the feeling of just sitting outside at a café relaxing. From a distance, I could hear music. I followed the sounds of drums and Spanish guitars to a cute little park where a few people were having a jam session. I was in awe. Before I knew it, my eyes were closed, and I was dancing in a circle to the music, letting it flow through my body. It was enchanting. It was as if the music completely took me over. When it stopped, I felt amazing, and I couldn't stop smiling. People were surrounding me and the folks playing, and they were clapping. It reminded me of the first time I performed on stage after my accident, and the crowd was cheering my name. That feeling was quickly matched when the guy playing the guitar told me to sit next to him. He pulled out another guitar and began teaching me. I felt like a giddy child every time I got it correct. I looked up at all the smiling faces and just embraced it. Could life truly be this simple and yet so pleasurable?

After a while, I said goodbye to the musicians, and I went back on my journey to find the beach. It wasn't long after that I did, but boy, it was warm out! They weren't kidding when they said, "The Barcelona heat will take you." I looked around at all the people enjoying themselves. I was a little shocked to see so many people walking around nude and in clothes. It was pretty cool. I wish everywhere could be like that, but in America, people would lose their freaking minds should someone stroll through the park nude.

I found a few stone seats, and I picked one with a footrest. I smiled at my surroundings then closed my eyes and just allowed myself to be engulfed in the environment. What was it about being away that made me feel so close to myself? The sounds of the waves hitting the pier drew me closer to it. I went over and put my toes in the water. It felt absolutely amazing. I have a theory that the sand acts as an exfoliate, scrubbing your sorrows away and the waves rinse your skin thus explaining why the ocean's water is so salty, leaving the person feeling refreshed and joyful. I was enjoying myself so much that I hadn't realized how badly my skin was burning. I took a look at my feet and remembered that I had a shoot coming up and that I should go back indoors for a little while, but just a few more moments were needed to just enjoy the scene.

Everyone was running around being so happy. There were a group of guys about 200 feet from me working out. I couldn't look away. They were goofing off and seeing who could do more pull-ups and such. I always find it amusing when guys start challenging each other, but I totally understand it. Challenges make us stronger. One of the taller guys kept looking back at me. "Uh-oh." I thought, realizing they were waving me to come over to them. I pretended that I wasn't curious and waved "hello." He walked over to me and sat beside me. "Are you going to join us?" he asked. I chose my words carefully and smiled. I said, "Or you guys could join me?" That's not at all what happened. He walked over to his buddies, and they all returned together. Suddenly I was being lifted into the air and carried like a hog about to be roasted on an open flame pit.

"Where are you taking me?" I asked. The one that approached me, Demetri, smiled and said, "Somewhere better than the workout area you're sitting in." He sat me down in front of a tiki hut, and a beautiful girl appeared. Much to my surprise, she was basically nude, but the guys didn't act any different than how they acted with me. I suppose that was the norm here. I found that to be pretty cool because she was absolutely stunning. She was slender, about 5'7, medium brown skin with almond eyes and blonde hair. Everyone was very friendly. She said something in Catalan then disappeared. When she returned, she returned with a round of Sammy Sosas. I knew this drink well since I drank several of them in the Dominican Republic. It tasted the way I felt - smooth, happy, and strong. I had completely forgotten about me needing to return to the flat due to my burning skin. I was enjoying my time with these adorable and naked strangers.

We ventured down the beach to a few little shops. I was really amazed that the girl, Nadia, was still nude. It almost empowered me to strip down...almost. We tried on little beach skirts. I told myself, "NO SHOPPING!" but it was so tough. Everything was so pretty. I found a top that would have cost easily 200 bucks in the States, but was only 27 euros in Barcelona. I wanted it badly, but I knew I had to budget for the rest of my trip. I had gotten down to the last of my reserves, and I wasn't about to tap out. A part of me wished that I hadn't purchased those key chains because I'd probably put them in a drawer and hardly ever see them again. A terrible habit of mine.

We walked over to an area where there was more live music playing. Demetri grabbed my hand, asking me to dance. I was stuffing my face with mango ice cream but conceded. The sun was starting to set, the drinks were kicking in, and the Spanish guitars were setting the mood. "You are Paradise." Demetri said. I laughed because it was such a cliché thing to say, but I fed into it a little and asked him, "Why?". To which he replied, "You have a unique spirit about you. There is more to you than what I can currently see. I don't know what, but I feel it. You are here for a reason, it's in your eyes." I stopped dancing because he had a very stern and serious look on his face. I walked us over to the beach, and I told him why I was here and about my entire adventure. Demetri listened attentively. He didn't speak for a while, and when he did, he seemed to choose his words carefully. "While it will be difficult to find your relatives here," he said, "I can take you to a place where the people could really use your heart." I told him I would like that very much.

He pulled me in close and held my hand, us both watching the sunset. It was so peaceful. It wasn't a "true" sunset because of where the beach was positioned, but it was certainly good enough. Demetri looked at me and asked me if I wanted to go to the place now. I didn't think twice. Of course, I wanted to go. I was a little concerned about getting into the car of another stranger, but my desire to see this place took over. I took a photo of the car and random map screenshots along the way to send to friend...just in case.

When we stopped driving, Demetri grabbed my hand and said, "Don't be afraid." Truth is, I wasn't at all...until he said not to be. I instantly began to think of what kind of trouble I had just put myself into. He walked around to my door and extended his hand. His entire mood had shifted, and so was mine. Where were we? We walked up to the door, and he spoke solely in Catalan. He asked me for my ID, and the people made a copy of it and took a photo of me. They then insisted on taking my cell phone. I refused so they agreed to take just the battery. I was feeling very on edge.

We were quickly ushered behind an invisible door then down a hall and told not to make a sound. This was it. This is how I was going to die, I was sure of it. Damn it, all those hostel movies I watched, and I still got into this guys car. What the hell was wrong with me? I kept looking around trying to scout a way out, but there was only one way in and the same way out. When we came through the door, there were 3 men in the front and 1 woman without any type of weapon, I'd struggle to get past all of them. I was almost too afraid to speak. Demetri had a very stern and focused face. I kept looking around the narrow, dark hall, trying to see anything that I could. I was considering all types of self-defense techniques that I could use while it was just the two of us, but then what? How would I get past the group of people in the office and why couldn't I make any noise?

Before I could ask any questions, Demetri and I climbed through another staircase, and I heard music. "It's okay to talk now." he said with a smile on his face. "Where are we? Why did they take my ID and try to take my phone? Where are we?" I demanded. "Princessa, take a look around." he said as he opened yet another door. Suddenly, a group of girls ran out, screaming his name. I watched as he lovingly greeted each of them. He grabbed my hand and introduced me in both English and Catalan. Almost immediately one of the little girls jumped into my lap. I couldn't help but smile, but that smile quickly faded as I noticed one girl off on her own. "Is she okay?" I asked him. "No," he said, "she's new here and doesn't trust anyone yet. We can't get her to eat or anything." I wanted to ask where we were again, but there was a brand on one of the older girls arms, and I knew exactly where we were. This was a safe house.

Knowing how this situation works, I now understood why we needed to be so secretive and quiet. It was all for the protection of these sweet girls. I decided to give it a shot. I walked over and sat beside the young girl, not saying a word. Instead, I grabbed a piece of paper and a crayon and wrote, "English or Catalan?". I set it beside her. Much to my surprise, after a while, she picked it up and wrote "both." I decided to keep it going. I figured being vocal might have scared her. We wrote little notes to each other for about 30 or 40 minutes. A bell rang, and she jumped.

We watched the other girls gather to get their food, but she refused to move. I then remembered a story another little girl told me about how the people that trafficked them would force them to do bad things or fight, and only the best person got to eat. My heart hurt for these young girls, but she needed to eat...she looked frail. I decided to use my imagination. I pretended to make a sandwich in the air, then eat it smiling and saying, "Yummm." She smiled when I pretended to make soup, and she pretended to add seasonings. I giggled and whispered, "I wonder what real food would taste like..." The young girl dropped her head. I was determined to get her to eat even if it took me all night. I stood up to go get a snack, and she grabbed my hand. "It's okay." I assured her. She walked closer to the food area, but stopped before we reached it. "It's okay," I told her again, "I will get it for you." I considered that she might have allergies and may not trust taking food from anyone so I turned my body so she could see everything I was doing then I set the tray at her feet and sat with her. She grabbed my hands and closed one of her eyes. I realized she was praying, so I asked the group if we could all pray with her. The girls gathered closely, but not too close to the child, and we prayed together then ate together.

When we were done, one of the younger girls handed her a doll. Much to our surprise, she accepted it. My heart was overfilled with joy. Suddenly an alarm went off. I realized it was time for me to go. My heart turned sad instantly. I wanted more time with them. When I went to walk towards the door, the young girl walked over to me and whispered, "Will you come back?" I smiled and told them all that I would return as soon as possible. The girls were giving me hugs and high fives. Demetri watches as I giggled with joy teaching them the "So Long, Farewell" song. The lights flickered again, signaling that it was their bedtime. Demetri and I took our leave back down the creepy and silent hall, back from behind the hidden door and out on the road where his car was. "Are you okay?" he asked. "Better than okay." I told him and thanked him for showing me. He told me I could come back tomorrow if I wanted and I absolutely did.

A little while later, he dropped me off at the flat. We walked to the door, and he grabbed both of my hands while looking me in the eyes. He had that focused look on his face again. "You are going to do significant things in your life." he said to me. "How do you know?" I asked. "Well," he replied, "you got that little one to not just eat, but begin to trust." He kissed my hands and told me goodnight. I went to bed thinking of all I experienced. My purpose...was this truly it? I'd always found my way to be around children and helping them. I'm not sure what was happening, but whatever it was...it felt right.

25

Finding Purpose

I woke up still thinking about the little princesses I met the day before. There must be something I could do, but if I could, didn't I have a responsibility to fix the same issues at home first? I feared people would be upset if I were off helping people around the world when the people in my own community were hurting, but that's the thing...I don't see it like that at all. I genuinely want to help whomever, wherever. I just want people to have food, a home, and be safe at the very least. I decided to get out of my head and follow my heart. Well, in this case, my stomach first.

I left the flat, walked down the street past the little cafés, and over to the big bridge where the beach was. It was a warm and beautiful day. I thought I would grab a sandwich, but the donuts stole my heart away. I sat in a beach chair, looking out at all the people enjoying themselves. "This is what life is all about." I thought to myself. I was still surprised by all the nudity. I didn't mind so much because no one was being gross or rude, but it wasn't the standard norm in the USA, so it certainly took me by surprise especially for boobs to be so close to McDonald's and other larger chains.

After a good 45 minutes of frying my poor skin, I decided it was time to head back inside until the sun went down. I knew it was warm in Barcelona, but I don't think I truly understood what that meant until I was four different shades. On the way back, I crossed another bridge. I came to a sudden halt when I saw the family before me. I dropped my head and proceeded to walk past, but I couldn't help but look back at them. "Were these people actually living here out in the open like this?" I wondered. It must have shown on my face because a woman spoke to me, "It's okay to be curious," she said, "some days are easier than others. " "Is this your home?" I asked, already knowing the answer to my question. "Yes," she said, "this is our home." From behind her appeared two children out of a fort and a man. My heart sank. Here I was gobbling down a pack of donuts and complaining about being sunburned, and these folks didn't even have a way out of the heat. They don't bother anyone, and usually during the day, they walk away so the tourist's feel okay crossing. The mother told me, "Sometimes people just leave food or coins. Other times, they don't. What we do is we keep it clean, so no one will bother us as we try to find work...but it can be very hard." It's almost (37 Celsius) 97 degrees here in the Spring.

The father pulled out some pots and plates. "Would you care to join us for lunch?" he asked. A part of me wanted to say "no" because I was feeling foolish, but they were so welcoming. It's incredible. These people had nothing, but were willing to share their nothing with me. So I stayed, and we made lunch while chatting. I asked them, "What can I do to help homeless people around the world, and what message would you like to give the world?" She said, "You can keep being kind to us and praying for us. Some like this lifestyle, many do not. It's not always a simple choice. I only ask that our children be respected and allowed to be in school." I was shocked. I did not know homeless children were not permitted to be in school; then I remembered you had to have a residential address to apply for school. The system is kind of funny that way. What sucks is if she went to the state for help, they would probably take her children away rather than offer a job. There must be a way to change that for our future.

I walked with the daughter to the gas station's bathroom to wash out the dishes. I decided to purchase a couple cups of ice and a big juice for them to share. I knew I didn't have much, due to my travel budget, but I wanted to pay back their kindness. After a while, I started to get ready to leave, then I realized the sun was setting. Unfortunately, on that side of Barcelona, you don't get a full sunset; however, it was just as good. I looked around and as tough as things were, I realized, "I am IN Barcelona sitting with these amazing people. This is truly what life was made for."

I said goodbye to my gracious hosts and headed back to the flat. Everything looked so different at night. I could hear the crowd that was coming and going to the big festival, Primavera. I wished I'd gotten tickets, but I was still just happy to be in Barcelona. The Cheetah Girl's song "Strut" began to play in my mind again. I couldn't help but smile. I found myself dance-walking the entire way back to the flat. By now it was quite dark, so I decided to put a little pep in my step, besides I knew I had a shoot early the next morning and no one likes baggy eyes.

When I arrived at the flat, my host was knocked out snoring. I smiled, quietly entering my quarters to process my day. I still couldn't get over that family I met. How easy could that have been myself or others that are so quick to merely pass them by? I wanted to change it all, but I knew I couldn't do it alone. I laid on the bed that night thinking of all the ways I could fix the little things. I decided I wanted to truly build a fostering home for those attempting to help themselves, but needing little assistance.

The past two days made me think about the things my siblings and I went through. Living in an abandoned house without heat and water...but now look. There I was across the vast ocean. I had gone to several of the top countries on my list, and my trip wasn't over yet. I really wanted to make the most of it. It still hadn't sunk in, with all my feelings, and I dare not even think about the return trip home. Tomorrow was going to be a good day, I just knew it. After all, I was going to a mysterious beach to shoot.

I woke up early the next morning to get prepped for the beach shoot. I wasn't exactly sure what to expect. I got in the car with my host, and we drove quite a ways away. As we were approaching the beach, I could smell the ocean. There is always something glorious about the water, it has a way of washing your worries away. We found a perfect place to park then made our way down the cliffs on to the beach. I took a look around and realized that I was the only one clothed. For a moment, I felt entirely out of place, but I soon realized that since it was a nude beach. No one would be gawking at me in my bikini while I was trying to shoot and I began to embrace my surroundings.

All of the rock formations were slippery and unique. The sand was a bit gravelly and pretty warm. I stepped into the water, closed my eyes, and began to pose for the camera. For a moment, I allowed the realization of this trip to wash over me and let it show through my images. Here I was, the girl who came from nothing, now shooting in Barcelona. The joy must have been showing because my host stopped shooting and just smiled at me. I was happy. I was excited. I was free.

26

When you least expect it

After getting my foot stuck, literally between a rock and a hard place, sinking deep into the sand as the tide raised, we decided it was time to wrap our shoot and get lunch. I spotted a little beach café, and we tried Pa amb tomaquet, a snack that Barcelona is known for. They are made from fresh and healthy ingredients. Barcelona is known for its delicious tomatoes, the use of olive oil into foods and the routine supply of sea products from the Mediterranean side. It was a perfect snack for me while we relaxed on the serene beach. People were sunbathing and playing in the Balearic Sea, though a particular couple caught my attention. The gave off newlywed vibes.

I watched as the guy snuggled the woman, feeding her fruit with his hands as she read a book. He slowly ran his fingers along her spine, caressing her curvaceous figure. I found myself in a state of desire. What must it feel like to be adored in such a public manner? I was reminded of the night I had with Laurent. Why hadn't I given in to those desires? I knew the answer to that question all too well. HIM...it's always HIM. I began to drift to a dangerous place in my mind. I started thinking of the time we spent together. If I allowed myself, I could still smell his cologne and feel his arms around me. Did I miss him, or was it the connection I perceived our relationship to be? This wasn't the time or place to have such thoughts. Thunder was rolling across the sky, and I agreed to meet Demetri tonight. I took the last sip of my drink and accepted that it was time to leave this piece of Paradise. We packed up the car and drove back towards Barcelona.

I sat quietly on the drive back. I couldn't shake the thoughts from my mind. I started to feel myself sinking, and there was nothing for me to grab on to. Gusto decided to drive me to the top of Barcelona, so I could see the entire city. It was stunning, but I was stuck and didn't know how to explain that to him. I still felt very uneasy with him, and my phone was completely dead. It wasn't as if Gusto ever did anything wrong to make me feel the way I did. I mean, there were times that I thought he was a little handsy. He had a habit of putting his hand on my knee when we were sitting in arms reach. It would send danger chills through my entire body. I didn't like it, but I also never told him, "No." I guess I had convinced myself that it was just a knee, but should that matter if it makes me uncomfortable?

Once we reached the flat, I promptly charged my phone to check for Demetri's message. Nothing. I was disappointed. I had actually been looking forward to getting together tonight and hopefully seeing the children again. I told myself that he was probably just working and would reach out soon. I decided to watch cartoons with Gusto. I felt like I was being rude by staying silent, unintentionally, of course. When I have a million things going on in my mind, I struggle to put them into words that others would understand, so I usually just keep it all inside. That is precisely my problem, I don't know how to let people know that I may be hurting.

I joined Gusto on the couch, and we watched a Spanish cartoon, and then a telenovela. Before I knew it, it was 8pm, and he'd passed out. I looked at my phone again. Just as I was preparing to accept that the night was ending, I got a text from Demetri, "Princesa, ha estat un dia de tristesa sense la vostra llum. Per què no il·luminem Barcelona? Vull mostrar-vos alguna cosa: mireu fora." I peered out the window, and there he was with wine and flowers. I smiled, pulled on a shawl, and quietly made my way to the street where he was waiting. Curious about the night, but refusing to over-analyze it, I made my way into the car. "The children want to see you one last time. I explained to them that this was your final night in Barcelona and I think we should make it your best." I agreed without reservations. It was something about the way he spoke that made me feel safe, but still filled me with adrenaline.

We drove back to the safe house. As we entered the 3rd door, the little one I had spent time with the visit before, we will call her Hailey, greeted me first. Hailey took my hand and led me to a bean bag chair, attempting to hand me a book. I looked around, and all of the children had on their nightwear. Demetri smiled and said, "They want to have a sleepover with you." I smiled, "Well if we are going to have a sleepover, we will need snacks, music, and beauty crafts." "Already 10 steps ahead of you." he replied, putting out a box of makeup, a variety of snacks and boom-box connected to an MP3 player.

The girls and I started to pull out the makeup as Demetri attempted to leave. "And where do you think you are going, sir?" I asked. "Well, I thought I'd let this be a girls night." he responded, but we were not letting him get out of facials and makeovers that easily. One of the older girls guided Demetri to a chair and proclaimed, "Ladies, we have lots of work to do." Everyone giggled and surrounded him plucking his eye brows, and pouring an avocado mask on his face. We put on a fashion show, then a talent show, and ended with a reading of "The Princess and the Frog." The story had neared its end when I looked around at all of the sleeping faces. Demetri checked his watch. "It is almost 2 am." he said. We started to put the girls in their beds, tucking everyone in. "I'm going to miss this." I admitted with a solemn realization that I would not be returning tomorrow night to play with the girls. As we were exiting, Hailey sat up and said, "Thank you. I will never forget you." She climbed out of bed, hugged me then went back to sleep. I felt the tears swell inside me. I knew I would miss the girls terribly. I wanted to adopt them all, but I knew that wasn't possible. Suddenly I was reminded of why I was on this trip in the first place. I had a mission to complete. I hadn't found my Paradise yet, but I knew I was forever changed.

We got back into Demetri's car. "Anaís," he said, "there is something I want to show you." We drove around a dimly lit Barcelona and parked the car. "Do you trust me?" he asked. Trust. Trust was such a foreign concept when applied to me. I don't even think I honestly trust myself. Perhaps that is part of the problem. I shook the thoughts from my mind. Reluctantly, I said, "I can try." Demetri put a blindfold on me, wrapped my arm around his, then led me out of the car and onto an adventure.

Though the mask blinded my eyes, my nose was working perfectly. I inhaled and proclaimed, "I smell Pinchos! And bread!! And, and DONUTS!!" He laughed, "WOW! Almost had it perfectly. You truly are a foodie." We walked a bit further, then he sat me on a bench. I could hear him fumbling around.

I took a deep breath and tried to listen to my surroundings. I could hear a car or two, but other than that…it was completely silent. I had begun to feel anxious. I had been blindfolded for what felt like 30+ minutes, which was too long for my comfortability. I could feel the anxiety rise as I recalled times of being locked in a dark room after hiding from my mother's boyfriend. I started questioning everything. Was this a good idea? Did I just put myself in danger? I wanted to respect Demetri's hard work to surprise me, but I was feeling overwhelmed with anxiety, and panic started to set in. This was a problem with HIM, too. He's tried twice to blindfold me and lead me to a surprise that he'd worked very hard on, but my anxiety always got the best of me. I had no reason to feel unsafe with HIM. He was, after all, practically my husband. That's didn't stop the fear and panic from setting in causing me to question him every step of the way, almost ruining his surprises.

"Demetri," I called out, "Demetri I.." "Here. I got you." he responded, taking the blindfold off me. "Sorry, I just- I tried." "You don't need to explain Princesa." he said, "I see how you are with the girls. It's okay. I understand." He pulled me in for a gentle hug, and I felt the anxiety begin to lessen. "Are you ready?" he asked. I nodded a yes. "Okay, turn around." he instructed. When I did, he revealed the picnic he'd laid out. Complete with candles, wine, pinchos (BBQ chicken on a stick), rolls, and much to my surprise warm eclairs. He handed me one explaining that Nadia was a great baker. "I figured with you returning tomorrow, this should make you feel a little closer to home." he said. "Home." I thought to myself. "Where was home now?" As if he could read my mind, Demetri lifted my chin where our eyes could meet. "That is a thought for another time. Look up." he said, pointing to a castlesque building. "Do you know what that is?" he asked. Before I could really think about it, "Strut" from the Cheetah Girls was ringing in my mind and immediately knew where I was. "You brought me to the Sagrada Familia?" I asked, looking him in the eyes. He smiled and took my hand. "Here, let's have a sit." he said, guiding me to his lap. "Is this okay?" he asked. Truthfully, I wanted to say, "No." but I couldn't. I appreciated how respectful he'd been, and I appreciated all his effort in setting up this beautiful night. I didn't answer him. I smiled and gave a deep sigh, allowing myself to sink into his arms. Demetri pulled out his phone, turning on a jazz station, and we snacked in silence. I was really enjoying myself, and I let my wall down, just a little.

"Princesa, have you ever been in love?" he asked. I felt taken aback by the question, but it was a fair question. "I think so…once." I responded. We spoke in detail about our lives, the good and the bad. I quickly realized that we had so much in common. I laughed at the story he told me of him being chased by pigs on his uncle's farm in Alicante. "Alicante," I voiced, "one day I will have to go there." Demetri sat up. He had that serious look on his face and kissed my hands. I am not sure why, but a little worry sat in. "I think it is time for your surprise," he said. I laughingly said, "Surprise? What do you call all this?" "A date, if that is okay with you?" he said, handing me a piece of paper.

"Calle Villegas, 56, 03001 Alicante (Alacant), Alicante, Spain."
"What is this?" I asked.

"That," he said, *"that is the address to your avi's business in Alicante."*

I looked down at the numbers. Tears fell from my eyes, and confusion filled my mind. *"But how did you get this? He's been dead for years, and my Abuelita lost the restaurant."*

"I went to get it today." he explained.

"From where?" I pushed, *"How did you find them, Demetri? You said it would be almost impossible."*

"Yes. I did. It would have been almost impossible for you. So I drove there last night after I dropped you off. " he answered. I was still confused.

"Demetri, are you saying that you drove over 8 hours last night to get an address?" I questioned.

"No," he responded, *"I drove 8 hours to visit my uncle and asked him to help me find your family. We asked around, and I met them—"*

"Wait, you met them?" I asked. I started feeling flustered. Why was he just now telling me this? I felt a mixture of relief, fear, and frustration. Apart of me felt like it was my journey to find them. I didn't want to be saved, in a sense. But I couldn't help but feel appreciative of his efforts. I told myself to calm down, then I listened as he recalled his encounter with my relatives. He told me how his uncle was able to negotiate a deal with the current owners of the restaurant and my Abuelita. They were able to agree to a partnership so it could be back in the family.

I was overwhelmed. "I hope I did not overstep. I am sorry for keeping this from you. I wanted to help. I ...its just that..."

Demetri struggled with getting his thoughts into verbal words for the first time in my experience with him. I could see the struggle in his eyes. What was going on? "Demetri, what is it?" I asked, pushing his hair back to reveal his hazel eyes. It was amazing how the green and yellow really showed under the embers of the fire's flame. His eyes met mine, and he grabbed my hands firmly. For the first time on this trip, I felt really afraid. I felt my body begin to tense up. I started thinking of ways to get away if he revealed something horrible.

"Anaís." he started. I inhaled deeply. *"Anaís, you are going to do amazing things in this world. You have this power in you that you are so obliviously unaware of. You have a purpose. That purpose will require certain sacrifices, but you will undoubtedly fulfill your purpose before you leave this earth."*

Tears started to fill my eyes. I felt something transition. I wasn't sure what it was, but it was a strong pull. The last time I felt this feeling was when I said goodbye to HIM.

He video called me a few days before I left. I was in Santa Monica sitting on the beach looking out at the vast ocean that lay before me, feeling my absolute worst. We had small talk for a while, then he told me he missed me. I laughed it off. "Can I see you?" he asked. But for what I wondered? We had tried and tried again. Was this just another "chat" where he'd make promises and advances that he and I both knew he had no intention of ever following through with? Yet, for some reason, I always let myself believe him - convincing myself that he meant it this time. I didn't bother to tell him anything that happened with Derek. I refrained from talking about my personal life with him at all. It was always too hard to fall into conversations that led nowhere. But we were in-sync. He knew something was wrong, even if I wouldn't tell him. That was why he called and why I answered. We had this strange bond that was as beautiful as it was toxic, but how many times do I have to get burned before I realize the fire is hot?

I hung up the phone and asked God, "What do you want me to do??" I sat in silence for a while thinking of HIM, my parents, and others I've trusted. The thoughts were getting me nowhere. I checked the time. It was 7:42 pm. Wanting just a little more time at the ocean, I put my headphones on and turned on my phone's radio. "From the Inside" by Linkin Park was playing. My heart sank. I felt broken. I couldn't think, and was barely breathing. I just cried and cried. "Breaking the Habit" followed by "Somewhere I Belong" played. I stood up and began my walk back to the flat. By the time I reached my bed, I was ready to collapse from the crying. I needed to just get away from myself. The darkness was taking over, and I was tired of feeling like this. I had left Santa Monica before when I went to Denver for a year, but something always brought me back to Cali.

I flopped onto my bed, feeling hopeless. My phone dropped from my hand, changing the playlist station. "I'm Moving On" by Rascal Flatt played. I hit repeat and must have listened to the song at least 5 times before I stood up. My path was clear...I needed to go and go now, but where? I closed my eyes and threw a knife at my poster of the world map. I stepped closer to see where it landed. "Paris?" I thought. Well, I was supposed to go the previous year to try to find my grandfather, but Derek's nephew came to visit and ended up staying with us.

The song was still playing as I opened my laptop to check my Facebook. "Cheap flights to Paris." was the headlining ad displayed on the screen. My phone rang, startling me. HE was calling me back. I told him I was considering leaving. When he asked when I planned on returning, I admitted to him that I wasn't sure that was in the plans. "You better come back. " he said , "You have to." "I'm Moving On" was still playing on repeat in the background. "That's our song." he noted.

I listened to the words:

"I'm movin' on. At last I can see life has been patiently waiting for me. And I know there's no guarantee's, but I'm not alone. There comes a time in everyone's life, when all you can see are the years passing by, and I have made up my mind that those days are gone."

"I have to go," I told him, "dinners ready." "Okay, I love you." he said. My heart always lurches when he says it. I so badly want him to mean it. No matter how hurt I am feeling, I always say it back. "I love you too. Goodbye." I hung up the phone, still listening to the song. I've said goodbye before, but my heart knew something was pulling me. I closed my eyes and allowed the words to wash over me.

"I sold what I could and packed what I couldn't, stopped to fill up on my way out of town. I've loved like I should, but lived like I shouldn't, I had to lose everything to find out. Maybe forgiveness will find me somewhere down this road. I'm movin' on."

When the song came to its end, I opened my eyes and booked the flights before I could talk myself out of it. 72 hours later, I was on a bus to NYC.

Demetri wrapped his arms around me tightly, and we laid there silently. A while later, the sun began to rise. I knew we should get up, but I wasn't ready. We heard a distant sprinkler awaken. "Princessa, unless you want a bath from the hose, we'd better get up." he joked. We smiled and stood to gather our things. Still a bit confused about Demetri's behavior, I remained silent as not to say anything awkward. Before I set off for his car, I stopped to marvel at the Sagrada Familia once more. "What do you think?" he asked."Such an incredible masterpiece that seems to only get better as she continues to grow." I said, still in awe of the magnificent cathedral. "Yes, you are." he whispered. I turned to face him, slightly blushing. He kissed my hand and led me back to the car. I had been having such a wonderful time with Demetri. To meet someone so compassionate, respectful, and adventurous is quite rare.

I had fallen asleep on the drive back to my host's flat. There was a different feeling in the air. An all too familiar feeling, but I wasn't ready to accept it. "Are you sure you don't want me to take you to the station?" Demetri asked. "No, you have work, and we have already been out all night, so I am sure you are tired." I responded. "Okay, but we will see each other soon." he persisted. Unlikely, but I smiled and hugged him goodbye. As always, he waited until I was inside and waved out the window before he drove off. Gusto was just waking up. "I got your note. I hope you had a good night. I am sorry I can't stay and chat, but I need to get going for work." he said, looking at his watch, "And you need to be getting to the station soon." We said our goodbyes and I began to pack my things. Within the hour, I called the taxi and set off for the bus station.

On the drive, I tried to recount my entire adventure, but I was so exhausted. The rain didn't help either. I had initially planned to walk to the station, but suddenly it started raining. By the time the taxi pulled into the station, it was pouring. I pulled my things out as quickly as I could and ran to check-in. Completely drenched, I walked around the station to find a snack. I grabbed a sandwich and headed for my boarding gate. I was taking the Flix bus back to Paris. It was going to be a 14-hour ride, but I didn't mind. I wanted to see the countryside anyway. "Barcelona to Paris – platform 6, now boarding." yelled the operator. "Finally!" I thought. I had been waiting to take off some of my layers and use them as pillows, but I was soaking wet.

"Do you need a towel, Princessa?" a voice from behind called. I turned around to be greeted by Demetri, Jordan, and Nadia. "We couldn't let you leave without a proper goodbye. My God, you are soaked!" she squealed. She removed her sweater and handed it to me, "I have many more. You need something dry." she assured me. I gave everyone hugs. "Last call. Barcelona to Paris – platform 6." yelled the driver. "I guess I better go." I said, slowly walking to the gate. Nadia and Jordan gave me another hug then went back to their car. Demetri followed me to the gate, helping me load my case on the bus. "Welp, that is it!" I said half-hoping Demetri would make a joke about me leaving my American life behind and becoming a gypsy as he joked when we first met. But he didn't. Instead, he hugged me, kissed me on the forehead, and said, "Fins a la propera vegada." I walked to my seat and looked out the window. He was still standing there, presumably waiting for the bus to drive off. As the driver started the engine. I let down the window yelling, "Fins a la propera vegada." blowing a kiss. He pretended to catch it very dramatically that made the elders behind me laugh. Then, off I went. Back to Paris.

As I nestled in my seat, ultimately preparing for a very long nap, I thought of Demetri, his friends, the children, then back to Demetri. He had been so kind as to go out of his way to help me. I know we said we'd see each other again, but I couldn't help but feel like this was the end. Could that be why he never tried to kiss me? Moments later, I began to drift off. I had two seats to myself, so I stretched out as best I could and allowed myself to completely fall asleep. When I awoke, I'd be in Paris...or a lot closer than I currently was.

27

The end is nigh...

I had slept for 9 hours straight and was still utterly exhausted. My back was hurting, and I needed a snack, so at the next stop I got off for a roam. I saw there was a little café with paninis. I reached into my pocket to grab some money, but instead, I pulled out a folded piece of paper. I quickly paid for my meal and went back to my seat to investigate the random note, wondering if it had always been in there. Immediately I was triggered into a memory flashback. I was in Colorado visiting a friend and preparing for a summit. I decided to wear a fancy red coat I owned. It was from before the chaos happened. I reached in the pocket to pull out the gloves that I had put in there earlier that day, when out fell a folded piece of paper. I opened it to reveal it was a letter from someone who had serious feelings for me. It took 2 months to find out that the letter had come from HIM. I allowed my friend, Julie, to convince me that finding the man who wrote the letter would mean I would find my true love. When we finally realized it was from HIM, I sat stunned for 20 minutes. How unfair and torturous life had been. Such a cruel joke to my heart.

When I got back to my seat, I opened the letter, and saw that it was from Demetri.

"Princesa, by the time you read this, you will be probably already in Paris. There is so much I want to say to you, so much I wish I said when you were in my arms, but I could not. You give so much of your soul to the world, it's time for you to receive some back. Remember what I said about you having a mission to complete, but it would require sacrifice? I meant that except in this case, the sacrifice would come from my soul. You are so pure. I have never met someone who genuinely wants to help the world as much as you. Watching you with the children, I knew I was in big trouble. If I am honest, I knew the moment we met when you decided to sunbathe in the workout arena. I thought to myself, "She must be new or very bold," little did I know that you were both. Anaís, I want you to explore the world. I want to witness your vision of a peaceful place for people to become a reality. Unfortunately, this means I have to put my desires aside for the greater good. I can tell that when you love, you love wholly and unconditionally. This is why I could not tell you that I have fallen in love with you when we were talking last night. It's too much of a risk. Should you felt the same, it could derail your entire journey. I will not likely meet anyone who made me feel the way you do. The love that you have to give is the love the world needs. It would be selfish of me to take it for myself, especially when you are on the cusp of greatness. I know you may not see it, but believe me when I tell you that you are going to impact this world in a monumentally positive way. I am honored to get to say that I have had a chance to experience a piece of Paradise with you. I will look back at our time together and revel in the knowledge that you have gone out and embraced all that you are. I pray that you continue your search for your Paradise and when you find her, please don't ever let go.

I will forever remember you.
With all my love,
Demetri

I sat there frozen. His words playing back in my mind, "I have fallen in love with you." How is this possible? I will admit there was most definitely an attraction that could have been built upon, but could it be love? How was he so sure I was going to leave a positive mark on the world? A part of me wished he'd just said it last night, but the more practical side to my mind knows that it would have changed the entire evening. For better or worse, I don't know, and now I may never know. I have a hard time opening my heart entirely to people, men especially. Perhaps he already knew this, and that is why he did not make a move.

I stared out the window, trying not to overthink the letter. It was pitch black except for the moonlight glowing on the snow upon the French Alps. I could see the stars. I tried to recount the constellations until I eventually passed out. It took forever for me to get there. I kept wishing I could fall back asleep, but that seemed impossible. 6 more hours to go, and it was as if my mind was Pandora's box, and it had just been opened. Everything started to sit in. The incident. The break-up. Derek. My heart started racing as I tried holding back the tears. I didn't want to be the weird girl crying on a bus full of people, but I couldn't help it. Everything I had locked away seemed to be fighting to get through and make its presence known. I pulled my blanket over my head and cried myself to sleep.

I woke up hours later as we were pulling into Pont de Levallois near Metro 3. I sat up, attempting to stretch, but my body had begun to lock up. I leaned back into my seat and looked out the window. "Okay..." I whispered to myself as I waited for everyone to get off the bus. I had finally reached the final stop on my trip. It was beginning to sink in. I could feel the anxiety swell in my chest. "Relax!" I ordered myself. I needed to focus and make my way to the hotel where I was meeting my friend from the Netherlands. I grabbed my case, texted Oliver, and got into a taxi.

The driver, Aaron, was kind. He attempted to make conversation, but he somehow knew my mind was overwhelmed. "Big decision aye?" he asked in an "I already know." tone. "Don't worry," he said, "you already know what to do. You just haven't told yourself, yet." The truth is, I did know, but it was complicated. I know what my heart wanted, but I also know what my mind thought the best decision was. As I was wondering if my heart and mind would ever meet, we were pulling up to The Westin Paris – Vendôme. I tried to tip Aaron, but he refused. "Keep your money, but follow your heart." he said. We shook hands then parted ways. I entered the Westin to greet my friend.

Oliver was much taller than I, with golden blonde hair and cool blue eyes. "Anaís, finally! I was thinking of sending the French guard to find you!" he joked. He promptly took my bags and hugged me. "It's going to be okay." he said. But was it, I wondered? He sat me down while he went to check us in. I was still tired, and the entire trip was starting to catch up with me. We had lunch in the café of the Westin while they took our things to the room. "So, you are staying in Paris?" he asked. "No." I said, but it came out as more of a question which made him give me a look. "But how can I? Don't I have responsibilities back in Santa Monica? I made commitments that I have to honor…but don't I have a responsibility to my heart too?"

I let out a deep sigh and finished my tea. Oliver was silent, just listening. He was good that way. Oliver and I met at a business conference in Texas. He was the media liaison, and I was one of the speakers. Over the years, we became good friends talking constantly. We both were on this trip to make a decision. His company relocated him, and now he was on the brink of a potential relationship that he wasn't sure he should give himself to. I often told him that there was nothing to be afraid of when it came to commitment, but I felt like such a hypocrite - considering I have a hard time giving guys a real chance. I'm not sure if I had a fear of commitment or the fear of lack of it.

I thought back to Laurent. I had such a great time with him, but I knew it wouldn't lead to anything productive, so I didn't allow myself to go further…but does everything have to be all or nothing? My mind instantly wandered to HIM. Was that our problem? I thought about the countless conversations I had with him. It was always the same thing. Me pretending to be okay with it just lingering in the air when, in reality, I wanted…no…*needed* a title. The title validated my presence to myself. It lets me know that I am making decisions with a purpose. "You're thinking about him, aren't you?" Oliver asked. I couldn't deny it. I dropped my head, feeling shameful. I was on the other side of the world, why was I wasting energy thinking about someone who frequently, unapologetically hurt me? Oliver squeezed my hand, and we retreated to the room.

The housekeeping manager opened the door to our room. "Et pour vous madame. Paris attend." she said, opening the French doors to the balcony and pointing. Our balcony overlooked the Jardin des Tuileries...filled with magnificent flowers. I turned to the right and there she was, The Tour Eiffel. To many, she was just a beautiful architectural masterpiece. For me, she was a representation of all things possible, my beacon of hope; my lady liberty.

On the balcony, was placed a vintage-looking bistro set. I sat watching the people below for a while. Some in a rush, others..not too much. It was a beautiful day. The sun was bright, with just enough clouds to not cause my skin to burn. I inhaled taking in the smells of a nearby patisserie. "You look so much at peace." Oliver said, walking over, "Come, let's go for a stroll." I grabbed my shoes and off we went walking toward the Champ de Elleyes. We took a tour of Paris visiting the Arch de Triumph then headed over to Ponte du Alexander iii. We eventually found our way to the love locks. I thought, "So many hearts put on display." Oliver saw me and gave me a nudge asking, "Hey, do you think you'll make one?" "Maybe one day." I said with a hopeful smile. "How do you think you'll meet the man that manages to hold on to Anaís?" he asked. I leaned on the bridge, looking out at the water. "I'd like to think it would happen somewhere memorable. Maybe I will be staring at the Mona Lisa, and he will accidentally brush against my arm. We both turn to excuse ourselves, but our eyes lock and in that moment; time stands still. I begin to blushingly smile, and the first words he will say to me are "Voudriez-vous avoir de la nourriture avec moi ?" and my heart would be his. "What does that mean?" Oliver asked. "Would you like to get some food with me?" I answered.

We both began to hysterically laugh. "Well, in that case, we should go visit the Louvre." he declared, guiding me down the road very quickly. "Okay, Oli-" I started still trying to catch my breath from laughing. "No time to chat, your true love is waiting for you with a bowl of pasta." he heckled, still briskly walking through a busy crowd. "Out of the way folks, true love is waiting!" he obnoxiously bellowed. He was a nut, but I was very amused. "Oliver, there is only one thing wrong with your plan." I told him. "Really? What then?" he asked, ready to have a rebuttal. "Well, darling. For starters, it is far too late to try to visit the Louvre. It is massive, and the lines would be exhaustively long. It's something we would have to start our day with if we wanted to see everything. And secondly," I continued pointing east, "the Louvre is over there...we are going in the wrong direction." Oliver stopped to contemplate these facts. "Hmmm. Right. Well, let us go to Notre Dame then. Maybe your true love waits for you at church." he said jokingly. We walked arm in arm, heading towards the Metro, set for the Bella Norte Dame.

Neither of us truly had the slightest clue where we were going, we were just following the wind. The Metro was rather crowded, as expected for late afternoon. There was a busker on the train playing "La Mer" when suddenly I felt a strong pull. Something was telling me to get off the train now! "Oliver, do you trust me?" I asked with a sly grin. "Oh, boy...you know I do. What are we getting ourselves into?" he said. "I don't know, but come on we have to get off the train right now!" I urged him standing up and heading to the exit. "Anaís, what is it? Slow down." he begged. I heard him, but I didn't stop. Something was pulling me, and it had a stronghold. "Anaís!" he called. Finally, I stopped to face him. "What is going on?" he asked, feeling very concerned. "I don't know, but let's keep walking. Just trust me." I told him. We walked only a little further to the opposite side of the train. "Wait!" I whispered.

"It's gone." "What is gone?" he asked feeling as confused as I, probably more. "The thing. The reason I got off the train. I had a feeling, but now it's gone!" I cried. "Oh, Anaís. I am worried about you. Maybe we should wait here for the next train. It will be only a few moments." he decided. We stood for maybe a moment or two before I turned around to face the statues behind us. "Oh mon Deiu." I said, dropping to my knees. Oliver turned in a panic to lift me, but then he saw it too. "Artemis." he read aloud. "Anaís, did you know she was here?" he asked. "No." I told him, staring at the statue. Artemis is the Greek goddess of the hunt, chastity and the moon. She eventually became known to be the protector of children. Artemis was and still is my favorite Greek goddess. You see, I had been obsessed with mythology since my 9th year in school. Their stories of passion, pain, and perseverance were a perfect metaphor for my life. We sat there in silence for a while. What was the universe trying to tell me? Before I could complete the thought, another train arrived. Oliver grabbed my hand and led me onto the train. I'd always felt a connection to the concept of the goddess. It was just amazing and strange the way something pulled me to her. I could feel the tears start to swell in my eyes, but I refused to be emotional in front of all those people. I took a deep breath, put on my sunglasses, pushing the thoughts and feelings to the back of my mind. I had told myself that there was a time and place for those things, and it wasn't right there.

By the time we arrived at Notre Dame, they were closing for the day. "Darn, I guess my true love will have to wait." I said, wrapping my arm inside of Oliver's. We opted to go back to the hotel the long way, which meant no Metros or maps. By the time we returned, it was after 10 pm and dinner time.

We looked over the menu, but I wanted something soothing. "Burgers and wine?" he asked willfully. I smiled, "Yes, burgers and wine." Realizing the time, I jumped up and screamed, "It's starting soon!!" "What is?" he asked, following me onto the balcony. "You'll see…" I told him, allowing myself to get excited. We sat with our food and wine, waiting. At a quarter to 11, the magic started. "Wow!" Oliver exclaimed. "Yeah." I whispered. The Eiffel Tower was shimmering. Nightly she put on these magical light shows for her viewers.

This went on until a quarter to 1, lasting only 20 minutes per hour. Oliver had long ago gone to bed. I chose to watch the towers light dance over Paris. I reached for my phone and considered calling HIM. I stared at the phone for a while. What would I say to him? Was this a good idea? I scrolled through my contacts and landed on my mother's name. I wondered if she even knew where I was. They would have forbade me from leaving to find any of our relatives. When I found out the truth about my grandfather, I was so hurt and angry. I promised myself that I would one day find him. The Eiffel Tower's final glittering display danced before she went completely dark. I blew a kiss to the moon and decided tomorrow I would start my search for my papa.

28

God Bless the Outcasts

I woke up to French toast and strawberries being brought into our room. I looked over at Oliver's bed, and he was already awake and working on his computer. "Hey sleepyhead." he said. I sat up and thanked the person delivering the food. "Eat up, we've got some work to do today." he instructed. I wasn't sure what he was talking about, but at the moment I didn't care. There was French toast, sausage, and strawberries in front of me, and I felt famished. After breakfast, I did my morning routine and checked my emails. "Oof." I thought. 2500 emails. I couldn't be bothered with them. I wasn't ready to deal with the world and their questions. I was still trying to deal with myself and my many questions. I closed the computer and began to get ready for the day.

We first stopped at a local newspaper. I decided that I seriously wanted to find my papa. I convinced myself that I needed to know where I came from before I could figure out where I was going. I put out an ad that read:

Do you know Deirdre Mayher? I am looking for my family. I am looking for a man named Rene with the last name Norgare.

I included my contact information and the only photo of Deirdre I owned. I had only met my gran once, and she was not a very welcoming woman. I hadn't known anything about how she and my grand-père met except that he existed and I was not permitted to seek him out. I was tired of being lied to, and I needed answers. I knew the ad was a long shot, but I had to try. I left, feeling somewhat hopeful.

Oliver and I decided to give Notre Dame another try. When we arrived, there was a massive crowd and a rather long queue, but we opted to stick with the wait. We moved past security thirty minutes later, and I was immediately enamored with its beauty. The stained glass windows had a unique charm about them. The ceilings were so high. I passed by the hall that led you to the bell towers. "God Help the Outcast" from The Hunchback of Notre Dame continued to play in my mind as I wandered around. I made my way to the "Prayer only" section and took a seat.

I hadn't been to church in years. I wasn't sure, sometimes, that God heard me, but there I found myself sitting and listening for him. "Please, don't make me do this alone." I whispered. I have struggled with my relationship with Christ for most of my life. Often, I wondered, if he'd been too busy to be bothered with me. I thought back to the times my mother and her boyfriend struck me unprovoked. I thought back to the time I jumped in front of my brother when my mother's stepfather attempted to strike him when I was eight years old. I went three weeks with a whelp and a cut, that covered the entire right side of my face and much of the left. There is still a reminisce of the cut on my face and arm. I thought back to the day my sister died; I felt empty, shattered, and I felt deserted. What kind of God would allow this to happen to innocent children? I grew up believing that I was mostly alone, primarily because it often seemed that way. It took time and growth for me to understand and accept that things happen for a reason, but that didn't mean it didn't hurt. My walk was better now, but many times, I felt my faith questioned. This was one of those times. Could he hear me? If so, when would he answer?

Oliver came to sit beside me. I knew he was ready to leave, so I said a quick prayer and lit a candle. On our way out, I took one more look at the stained glass window behind the altar. "I'm still listening." I whispered then turned to the exit. I then walked Oliver over to Montemarte so he could see the Sacre' Couer. I decided to wait at the bottom of the hill since my leg was starting to bother me a lot. I found a nearby bench and checked my phone. 16 new messages. I opened a few, one being from Laurent. We chatted a little over the last few weeks. I wasn't really sure what to say to him. I am in a different mindset since we last saw each other. Part of me believed I got caught in the magic of Paris, and that is why things got so "wild" between us. I still hadn't told Oliver about that night primarily because I knew exactly what he would say. "Are you crazy? Anaís, you are in Paris! Call that boy and SIT ON HIS FACE!!" he'd tell me while trying to find Laurent's number. Oliver and I have vastly different views about sexual relationships. He was a wild child, ready whenever and wherever. I sometimes wished I could be more like him and just let go. Unfortunately, that is not ideal by the societal standard for women.

I continued to check my updates, switching apps to check my emails. HIM had sent one. Reluctantly, I opened it and almost immediately regretted it. The email didn't say anything. Instead, included a dozen or so photos of him and I from our previous years together. Why was he doing this to me? More importantly, why was I allowing him to? I turned off my phone and put it in my purse. Moments later, Oliver returned very excited about having explored the Sacre' Couer. I assured him that he must see it at night. "Oh, yea? When did you see it?" he asked. I could feel my cheeks burning from blushing. "Ohhh. There is a story, then?" he continued. I promptly changed the conversation. "Oh, look! A chocolatier! Let's check it out." I giggled and bolted down the hill and into the shop.

The shop was absolutely amazing! There was a replica of Norte Dame, and the Eiffel Tower sculpted in pure chocolate. I was in heaven. We each purchased our choice pieces then headed back for the Metro towards the Eiffel Tower. I remembered climbing on the first day of this adventure, so it was only fitting that we climbed as the journey came to an end. When we finally made it to the top, Oliver was in familiar awe. "I know right?" I said as he stood, staring out across the La Sien. "I'm not ready to leave." I confessed. "Where do you want to go?" Oliver asked, half already knowing the answer. I pretended to ponder then shouted, "VERONA!" A few people looked at me like I was crazy. Oliver and I laughed, running to find the lift and leaving the Eiffel Tower. "You know we can't go, right?"Oliver exclaimed. "Yea…but it's a nice thought." I said, rather disappointed. We took a walk toward La Seine and sat down. "Have you decided what you are going to do?" he asked. It was time for me to be realistic with myself. "I am afraid to leave this place. I feel such peace here, and I am worried that if I leave, I won't ever come back. I don't want to lose what I have found." I replied, "But I know I have responsibilities in Santa Monica too." We sat and just listened to the water. Today was my last full day in Paris. Tomorrow

Oliver and I would have lunch after my meeting with an artist, then we would part ways. He returning to The Netherlands and I to the States. I wasn't ready, but it was time. As much as I didn't like it, I had bigger demons to battle, and I couldn't run anymore.

We went to find dinner then started to pack for our trips back home. Oliver stepped out to find a luggage cart, but when he returned, I'd disappeared. "Anaís?" he called, "Girl, where are you? I've gotten the cart. Anaís?" Moments later, my phone rang. "Crap." I whispered. Suddenly the doors to the wardrobe that I'd climbed to were opened. "You know, closing your eyes doesn't mean I can't see you." he announced. I put my head down. "Besides," he continued, "your toes were sticking out." He grabbed my toes, and I started to giggle. "Why can't I stay?" I asked, already fully knowing the answer. "Because you are a strange woman that puts the world before herself." he replied curtly. "Olly!" I said, half surprised. "What? You know it's true!" he said, putting my things on the trolley. I reached for his hand. "Olly." I called. He turned to look at me. It was as if he was perfectly reading my mind. "You want to see it one last time. Here, let me put our things in the taxi, and we can stop along the way."

We loaded up a large taxi and headed down Rue de Rivilo and onto Place du Concord towards the Tracadore. When we arrived, I walked the stairs facing the tower. I took a seat, closing my eyes and just breathed for a bit. I wanted to take in the last bits of peace I felt before returning to the States. After a couple of moments, I walked back to where Oliver was waiting for me. Before entering the taxi, I turned to the tower and whispered, "Je reviendrai." Blew a kiss to the sky and went to the airport. The drive was silent. I started to allow myself to feel numb to the pain of leaving. My heart ached, but I knew I made the right choice. After all, there was a bigger demon haunting me, and it was time I faced it.

29

Journey to the past

When I returned to Santa Monica, a part of me felt invigorated. I had actually taken off for several weeks and just adventured. I was proud of myself. I needed it so badly, especially with what I was about to deal with. No one knew, not even HIM. For a few months now, I had been experiencing severe health issues. I already had a significant history of health complication; including ovarian cancer. It was almost the end of summer, and I just wanted to get through my birthday without having to deal with everything. For the next four months, I went on with life as nothing ever happened. I left most of my things in storage and stayed with a friend. A month later, I woke up to a lady screaming in French at 4:37 am Santa Monica time.

"What in the hell was happening?" I thought. *"Oui?"* I answered, still trying to collect my thoughts.

"est-ce Anaís Bouvier?" she asked.

"Oui, Madame. Comment puis-Je Vous aider?" I asked, trying to wake up.

"Vous êtes américain?" she questioned.

"Oui." I answered, wondering what this was all about *"Parlez*

vous Anglais?"

"non désolé," she replied. Then there was a shuffle.

"Hello, hello. Can you hear me?" what sounded like a young boy asked. *"I am Henry. I*

work for Madam. I am looking for Anaís Bouvier. Is this you?"

"Yes. That is me, What is this about?" I asked.

"You are the daughter of Deirdre Maher?" he asked. My heart started racing. Who was this

person calling me at 4:30 in the morning, asking me about my gran. "This had better not

be a prank." I thought to myself.

"Oui_yes...well No. Deirdre Maher is my grandme're." I said

"Oh! C'est magnifique! Madame is your, how do you say, other grandme're. She was married

to René Borde for many many years!" he told me.

"Borde? Hold on. You said, 'she was.' What does that mean?" I asked. Anxiety filled my

chest. I was now sitting upright, and my hands were shaking. Had it worked? Did I find

my family?

"I am sorry, Mademoiselle. Monsieur, René crossed on this past march." he explained.

My heart started aching. I knew there was a chance of this, but I wasn't ready to hear it.

The ultimate dead end. What is worse than having no information is having information

that leads you to nowhere.

"Mademoiselle Annalise would like to meet with you. Is this possible?" he requested, but it

was not. She was there…"Wait, where is she?" I wondered.

"Where are you? What city and country?" I asked

"We are in Paris, France." he retorted, *"Where are you?"*

"I am in Santa Monica. I am in the United States. May I ask, how did you find me?" I

questioned. Was this really happening? Had my family, well sorta, been so close all

along? I'd begun to wonder if we ever passed each other on the streets.

"Your picture in the paper, of course. Madame always reads the paper, just as Monsieur René

had every day." he responded matter of factly. I had to admit, I was slightly jealous of

this man. He knew so much about my grand-père, and all I ever knew was that he

existed.

"Oh, I see." thinking to myself, "Duh, Anaís. You have ads for the next 12 months." *"Well,*

I cannot come right away to visit, but I would like to speak to her." I requested, but

something struck in me. What if these people were frauds? *"I mean no disrespect,"* I

started, *"But how do I know that you are who you say you are? I have birth papers, but what*

do you have?"

"One moment, Mademoiselle," he requested. I could hear voices in the background but

was struggling to understand what they were saying. A few moments later Henry

returned to the phone. *"Madame wishes to tell you of your families origin. She has*

photographs, but you will need to come to Paris to see them. There is a problem, but not to

worry, I will help. Madamoiselle speaks very little English, but not to worry. Henry will
   translate if you like."

Annalise and I spoke for hours. It was almost 11 am my time before we said our goodbyes, agreeing to meet when I returned to France. I had learned so much about my family. There were undoubtedly some dark secrets that made everything start to make sense.

The gist of their story I got was well, born in 1938, René Borde was a spirited young man, very much a hopeless romantic. René met Deirdre Maher in the summer of 62 while on holiday in Paris. Already in a relationship, René kept close, but "distant" friendship with Deirdre as to respect boundaries...but as one can imagine being in the '60s in France, in their 20s among protests and war...they still found their "sparks" inflamed.

It took some time for René and Deirdre to be together, partially because she lived in Ireland, which during these times, it wasn't particularly advisable for travels...but that didn't stop them. René decided to make way to the southern regions of Ireland for a short period.

By the late '60s, the two had basically become one. Their families disapproval wasn't enough to stop them, René and Deirdre began what would become considered a long engagement. Much to Rene's surprise, in the spring of 1970, Deirdre decided to break the engagement and set on for America. 2 years later around Deirdre's birthday, she found herself on holiday in Ireland. Having already met a man, Steven, in the States and married him... Deirdre had clearly moved on from René...or, so they thought. On a not so special day, Deirdre found herself in Paris wandering the shops when she heard a man call her name from behind, "Deirdre?" She knew that voice all too well. So well that she wouldn't even turn to face the man. "Deirdre, look at me." René said. When she turned to face him, his eyes swelled with tears. There she was after all that time, but why? The two spent the day talking and catching up. To René, it seemed like no time had passed at all, but time had indeed passed. Deirdre still hadn't told René that she was married. This became problematic when René and Deirdre found themselves in each other's arms. For two and a half weeks, the two were inseparable. In René's mind, it was like nothing had ever changed.

On a rather bright night, the two walked the streets together in Paris. Walking along the River, the two talked as they always had when they were younger, laughing and making jokes, you would not have ever known there was quite the amount of chaos around France. In a rush of faith, René looked at Deirdre and said, "I think it's time we got married, don't you?" She turned to face him down on his knee asking her for her hand, René still didn't know Deirdre secret. Deirdre smiled at René. Unknowing the dark truth, René told Deirdre, "Meet me at home. I have a surprise for you." He set off to meet a friend who was late delivering a ring René made for Deirdre. Much to his dismay, when he returned home with a bottle of wine, flowers, and the ring...Deirdre was gone. All that was left was a note saying, "Goodbye." René's heart was shattered. It seemed history was repeating itself. René hadn't a clue as to where she'd gone; naturally, he went to her parents home to seek her out. Feeling rather, begrudged at the thought of René even asking for Deirdre's hand, her cousin informed him that she was now living in the States and provided an address, so that's exactly where he went. For the first and only time in his life, René crossed the ocean and went to America, what he found...the words could not explain. He walked up to the door, took a breath, and knocked. Opening the door was a tall African American man named Steven. It was a bit shocking considering it was the 70's...but what came next blew his mind and his heart.

René said, "I am here for Deirdre Maher. Does she live here, sir?" "No, but Deirdre Crosby does. What is this about?" "Who is it, baby?" called Deirdre from behind. "Baby?" thought René..."Did she say, 'baby'?" But the word was nothing compared to the next shock. Stepping out onto the porch, Deirdre's body revealed that she was very pregnant. "Do you know this man?" asked Steven to which René quickly replied, "I'm an old family friend. They told me your family now lived here. I wanted to have a visit before I returned home." Steven looked curiously as René, then kissed Deirdre goodbye. He was going to be late for work if he didn't hurry and the foreman didn't have that.

Finally alone, the two stood silently on the front porch. Rene' couldn't stop looking at Deidre's belly. "A baby?" is all he was able to say. Deidre replied coldly, "And a husband too." In all the shock, René hadn't noticed the humble ring on Deirdre's finger. He looked in Deidre's eyes, apologized for dropping in and left without another word. René never returned to the States again. He often thought about Deidre and the child, but it was a child with her husband...or so he thought.

It wasn't until 2008 that he learned the truth. At this point in his life, René couldn't travel. He made efforts to find Deidre and the child, but with no records of Deidre Maher (Deidre had changed her last name upon moving to the USA to 'Brooks'), he didn't stand a chance. With only a photo provided out of spite from one of Deidre's relatives, René Borde died March 13, 2017, never having met his daughter or grandchildren. How interesting fate would have it, that the Spring of 2017, Anaís Bouvier (René's biological granddaughter) would come seeking a lead to her family?

The irony of the situation was that I grew up speaking English and French, but mother would tell me, "We speak English here." and for the most part…I only spoke English, and I 100% rejected my accent. I never knew where it came from, and it always got me into trouble. The most astonishing thing about my families history is my grand-père's younger sister was my first grand teacher, Ms. Norgare! I began to have flashbacks of being in Ms. Norgare's classroom. She always encouraged me to speak French, I just thought it was a literature thing. She knew what life was like for me growing up. While there was nothing she could do to get me away from my mother because I couldn't leave my brother, she kept in contact as best she could. She's the one who told me when I was in 8th grade that I was French. She (illegally) did a genealogy exam on me. It was her way of encouraging me and showing me that I did have a history. Intercultural days were the worst for me. I'd always sit in the back of the room. Alone. Feeling like I didn't belong anywhere. All anyone ever told me was that our family lived in Santa Monica, and that was all that mattered.

In high school, I had an incident with my theater instructor, who was the only person who knew that I spoke french. I told her about Ms. Norgare and everything in a mini-breakdown I never saw Ms. Norgare again. I didn't know why…until today. In 2015, I was very serious about finding relatives. I met my gran, Deidre. In an attempt to bring her up to date about my life from 1st grade to current, my gran slipped and said, "That woman should have never been allowed to be an educator." as I was telling her of my favorite teacher. I rebutted, "What a peculiarly hateful thing to say about a person you don't even know!" "I know her, alright! That woman was a snake who never could mind her own business!" My gran said, slamming her glass on the table. I didn't like the way she was talking about one of the kindest people I had ever known.

It was then that I found out who "that woman" was. "She was as much as a loony as her ridiculous brother. Going on about love. What was love going to solve?" She went on, "Love will have you in the poor house child. 'Love' certainly wasn't going to feed your mother!" She froze dead in her tracks. She'd said too much, and I heard every bit of it. "What does my Mother have to do with this man and Ms. Norgare?" I asked. "Nothing. You need to be going. I have things to do." She said as she attempted to push me out the door. "No!" I yelled, "You tell me or I will ask my mother!" I said firmly, refusing to give up on the subject. "You wouldn't dare." she challenged glaringly. "Try me." I replied, matching her tone. "He was the man I was with before Steven." she revealed curtly. "But what does he have to do with my mom?" I urged, but I knew the answer to my question as soon as the words left my mouth.

I stood there in shock. She had just admitted that Steven, the pedophile, was not my grandfather. Well, in not so many words. She refused to give me any further information and forbade me to look further. She threatened, "You will destroy several lives if you don't keep this to yourself." She then told me to never come back. But why would I with how horrible she treated me? Knowing what I know now, everything Deidre said made sense. Annalise explained the reason I never saw Ms. Norgare again was because my mother and gran had a restraining order placed on her to keep away from us when she showed up at the house once requesting to meet with my mother. I felt a little sick. I had so many questions. Why keep all of this a secret and most importantly, why didn't anyone come to get us while we were being abused? I felt my temper flare-up. I told Annalise that I didn't want to hear anymore, but I didn't mean it. "I have but one more question for you." I asked coldly, "If family was so important to him and if he was such a great man...why didn't he ever come back? Why didn't he stop them from hurting us?" There were so many adults that were in and out of our lives, yet not one attempted to save us from our mother's cruelness.

Annalise apologized for the pain I've felt. She then explained that though she had her suspicions, Ms. Norgare had zero evidence that my mother was René's child nor that I was his grandchild until she did the DNA test on me. I couldn't understand. Ms. Norgare was kind to me for as long as I can remember. "Why would she be so nice to a random child?" I asked, feeling even more confused. "Because your mother looked exactly like her brother." she stated. "Anais," she tried to explain as best she could, "you must understand that the laws are so different between the two countries. Without evidence, there is nothing anyone could do. Your grand-mère had her name changed before she married the man you grew up believing was your grand-père. As far as anyone was concerned, she did not exist. He tried for years to find Deidre. He even contacted Steven. "They divorced. He was an abusive psychopath and pedophile! She is now married to someone else who does not like people of color!" I belted out with tears streaming down my face. "It still doesn't make sense, why didn't he come for us. We would have left. He would have saved us!" I cried out. I was frustrated. I had finally found my family, and he was gone.

The pain struck so deeply. Annalise confessed that when René finally found Deidre, she refused to tell him where my mother was and urged him to not disrupt my mother's life. Deidre told him that if he did not stay away that she would file a protection order and have him sent to jail. René had no idea of the torment we were enduring, and Deidre kept it all a secret. Sadness and confusion turned to rage. She knew! My gran knew this entire time and chose to keep it from me. I could've had a family. I could have been loved and protected. All I could do was cry. "Ma douce enfant," Annalise said, "please do not weep. Things will be better now. You have me if you like." I was very appreciative of the offer, but I needed time to process. I thanked her for speaking with me. We agreed to meet during my next visit, and we hung up the phone. I decided that the day was already too much for me and I went back to bed.

I laid there, trying to process all the information I have been given. I had a grand-père who loved and wanted us. I had a gran who I spent my life hunting down only for her to turn out to be the devil reincarnated. I no longer wanted anything to do with her. It was clear that Deidre did all she did for the sake of survival, but she was her only true interest. I had an aunt that I couldn't find. Ms. Norgare's first name was actually Marla, and she was the best friend of Annalisè growing up. It's crazy! My entire life…my favorite teacher…was actually family…and she was there in Chicago for so long. I asked Annalisè was there a way to find Marla, and she said, "No, they never had children." Marla Norgare and Annalisè are sisters-

JOURNEY TO THE PAST

in-law. Marla married Annalisè's brother, who died in the war a couple of years before she moved to the States. 15 years after René returned to France from facing Deidre, he and Annalisè married; remaining married through his death.

I started remembering little things about Ms. Norgare. When I knew her, she was a fierce woman. I very much looked up to her. She was very strong…kinda loud and scary at the same time. She always told me, "Stand up straight. Look sharp." and always called me her little "Colombe", which translates to "dove" in French. She never called me by my name so on the rare occasions that I would hear her say, " Anaís!" I'd bolt right up. Ms. Norgare was also the one who put a book of poets into my desk, creating my love of writing and art. As crazy and messed up as it all is, my life makes so much sense to me now. It also made sense why we couldn't find anything but dead ends when we first started our search. I kept looking around for "Norgare", but my grand-père's last name was actually Bordè. I wonder what Oliver would have thought about all of this, but that phone call would have to wait. I needed more time to process. I needed to rest.

30

The truth finds it's way

Life had been crazy since the call with Annalise. Another 2 months had passed, and I was obsessed with finding out more information. December was inching closer and so was the winter summits. I began to plan my summit season out. I had been speaking to Annalise a few times a week since her first call. She even figured out how to Skype, and she emailed me a photo of my grand-père. She was right - he and my mom did look just alike. I was practicing my presentation on Annalise when I doubled over in searing pain. If this were a Twilight Series, I'd swear that a vampire had just bitten me and I was transitioning. I managed to reach my emergency button from when my heart failed a few years ago. Twenty minutes later, the medics were rushing me to the hospital.

Everything was blurry, and the inside of my mouth tasted like metal. I would have been a lot more scared except I knew what was wrong. That is why it was no surprise when the doctor told me the cancer was back and was trying to spread. The truth is, the cancer returned around Easter of 2015 and had simply decided to remind me of its presence...as if I could ever forget.

I had the doctor explain to Annalise what was happening. Apparently, she had been ringing my cell phone off the hook for the past two hours I was getting x-rays. The Oncologist asked me what I wanted to do. I told them the same as I told other doctors, "Chemo is not an option…I can't do that again." I convinced myself that I would just have to deal with the pain and learn to live with it. I mean, how much worse would it get? But I was not prepared for that answer. After 5 days in the hospital, the doctors and I had to confront the fact that the cancer was and had significantly progressed to what they called Stage 4. Stage 4 cancer means the cancer had spread from where it started to another body organ. This is also called secondary or metastatic cancer. It's about as bad as it can get before it is deemed terminal, something that had become a real possibility for me. "Viens à la maison, s'il te plaît?" Annalise asked. She explained that she had some friends who were doctors that might be able to help me. At the time, I was feeling very pitiful. I was tired of being sick. I was not only feeling trapped in the world around me, but also within my body. Just when I thought it couldn't get any worse, the doctors told me the likelihood of me surviving another surgery was about less than a 30% chance.

Things were officially scary. I spent the next two months working out a plan. My life was already complicated enough. It didn't make sense for me to tell anyone and cause panic over something none of us had any control over. Annalise had found me a doctor that would be willing to do the risky laparoscopy. Our biggest concern was my heart giving out while I was under anesthesia. I decided to put everything I owned back into storage. I wrote out a will, and I accepted that I may not ever return again. As far as the public knew, I was going off on my annual summit. I decided that I would tell the people that needed to know what was happening closer to the surgery date. I felt like I had to do this on my own, or I wouldn't go through with it. There was a high chance that the cancer would evolve to stage 5, but there was a greater chance that I would not survive the surgery. Telling my peers meant they would, understandably, try to talk me out of this or everyone would get emotional about the entire situation. I didn't need that. I needed to be in the right mindset walking into this battle. It was finally time for me to face my biggest demon.

On Feb 5th, I went to NYC for the start of my summit. What had usually been an exciting affair for me, had become void in the context of where my life was potentially headed. The world saw my work and a smile on my face, but no one knew that I was dying on the inside; both literally and figuratively. Day after day, the ordeal had become more and more real to me. I was staying with my friend, Cory, for the week. She was a tallish, American-born Indian girl. We frequently went out for snack adventures, but rarely had time to just sit around and chat. Cory had a new boyfriend, and I wasn't the biggest fan of him. He hadn't necessarily done anything wrong, I just felt like I needed my guard up around him.

When I headed to Manchester on the 13th, the sadness tried creeping in. Naturally, the world had gone Valentine's Day crazy, and not to anyone's surprise, I didn't have a date. Prior to boarding the plane, an ambassador was offering fireball shots. Against my better judgment, I took not one, but two. "Eh, what the hell. I can't drink after this weekend anyway, and I may not even be around after this." I grimly reminded myself wolfing down both shots before getting the boarding queue.

Boarding was nauseatingly slow, per usual. I took my window seat, hoping no one else would sit next to me...but I was wrong. Both seats got taken. The middle by a girl with a short, sporty hair cut and the aisle by a very tall guy that didn't look to be much older than I. The middle seat girl and I both giggled at the dysfunction of the aisle seat boy. He seemed a bit unorganized to a typical person, but I saw right away that each of his bags was carefully packed according to his immediate needs. All of that organization went out the window when his bags toppled on him.

Shortly after the plane took off, my stomach threw a fit. I had dozed off for what had to be like only 15 minutes. I was abruptly awakened by a sharp pain in my stomach and a heaviness in my chest. "Oh, fuck!" I thought. Unfortunately, I had drunk at enough parties to know exactly what was wrong with me. I bolted up, climbing over my seatmates and squeezing past the flight attendant. I couldn't see anything. Not only was my sugar dangerously low, but the fireball was also not sitting well with my current conditions. Why the hell did I think fireball in my body, literally right before I was boarding, was a good idea? When I finally made it to the back of the Dreamliner 787, I almost passed out trying to explain to the attendants what was wrong. One caught me and got the bathroom door open for me.

After purging everything in my tiny body, I sat in the back with the attendants for an hour to make sure I would be okay for the remainder of the flight. When I felt like the coast was clear, I freshened up then returned to my seat. Middle seat girl was trying not to have anything to do with me (though I couldn't blame her much). She quickly moved her seat as soon as I returned. All that was left were aisle seat boy and me. "Are you okay?" he asked. "Yes, I think its all better now. Thank you." I weakly responded. The truth was, my insides were killing me. It felt like someone had used me as a punching bag for the last hour.

"I'm Adam." he said, extending his hand. "Anaïs." I replied. We shook hands. Little did I know that was the start of an interesting ordeal. Adam and I talked the remaining 6.5 hours of the flight. "I have to know. What are you writing in that book?"I asked, trying not to appear too nosy. "Okay, don't laugh, but it's my to-do list. I can't explain it, but I have to have it." he responded. I stared at him blankly then burst out in laughter. "Oh, come on! I thought you weren't going to laugh!" he joked. I smiled at him then pulled out my very own notebook full of to-do-lists. He too began laughing. "What are the odds?" he asked, still smiling. We had about 3 more hours left on our flight. "Oh, you must be exhausted. Maybe you should rest." he said. He began to move my leg across his. I leaned my head on my pillow that was leaning on the window, and Adam leaned his head on my shoulders. Before I knew it, we were both sound asleep.

When we landed, Adam asked if he could have my number. I didn't have a reason to say no, so I obliged then we went our separate ways. I texted my host, Mitch, to let him know that I was on the way, and I started for the exit. The major problem was, I couldn't remember how to get out of the terminal and on to the train. I looked at my phone, and it was after midnight. "Fuck." I thought, "Everything will be closed too." Ready to just call it a night and camp out at the airport, Adam walked up. "Hey, did you figure out where you are going?" he asked.

I didn't want him to know that I was lost, but I also knew it wasn't a time to be prideful. "Yea, no. Do you by any chance think you could tell me how to get to Culver St.?" I asked. He pulled out his map, "Oh yea. I know where that is mate, but you're going to have a hell of a time getting there tonight!" He explained that the train I needed to be on, the last train for the fastest route was arriving soon and I hadn't yet gotten a ticket for it. "Well shit," I thought "alright Anaís, what are you going to do?" but before I could start to sort my plan out Adam offered to guide me. "So it's the opposite direction, but I don't mind escorting the lady...if you wished?" he offered with a smile on his face. We grabbed trolley tickets and off we went.

He wasn't kidding when he said it would be tough. We took 2 trains, walked 11 blocks and waited 2 hours for the bus that would take me directly to my host's flat. It didn't help that my phone was now out of service and roaming hadn't kicked in yet. We tried to find food, but not even McDonalds was open. We ended up just huddling on the stoop of a local business. It was freezing in Manchester, and I did not have enough layers on. "Would you like my jacket?"Adam offered. "But what will you wear?" I replied. "Eh, it's okay, I'm used to this weather." he said, putting his coat around me. "Why was he being so kind?" I thought to myself. Also, why was I always so suspicious of kind people? He was so sweet to pull my massive suitcase, so I decided to carry one of his smaller bags. I accepted his coat, and we waited for the next bus. Two hours later, he put me on the bus and told the driver where to remind me to get off.

I was so tired that as soon as I arrived at Mitch's flat, I passed out and slept into the mid-evening of the next day. When I awoke, I had a few messages. One of them being from Adam. "Can I see you again?" I was surprisingly delighted to hear from him. I suppose he was a healthy distraction from what this trip was really about. We agreed to meet in 30 mins in downtown Manchester. Unfortunately, without Wi-Fi, I got lost and had no way to contact him. I was very surprised that he was still there, waiting for me when I arrived almost 2 hours later. "Oh, I am so sorry!" I explained why I was late and offered to treat him to a beer. We popped into a local pub for a bite to eat then set off on a late-night adventure.

Arm in arm in the pouring rain, Adam showed me the city. We walked around Castlefield. It was too late to go inside the gallery, but I was still having a great time. It honestly reminded me of London. So many tall buildings that were quite modern looking, but there was still a lot of charm left to the historic city. We went to city hall that looked like a replica of Big Ben. I marveled at the neo-Gothic architecture. "I am going to take you somewhere special that I think you will very much like." he said, refusing to give me any hints. I liked the way he smiled so innocently. During our walk, we talked about life and our purposes. He seemed so unaffected by the chaos of the world. I admired that about him.

A while later, we arrived at the Manchester Cathedral. "Remind you of anything?" he asked. It sure did, Paris. Notre Dame to be exact. While it wasn't modeled after it necessarily, it certainly carried its charm. Unexpectedly, a bell went off. "What was that?" I asked, a little startled. "It means its midnight, don't tell me Cinderella has to go so soon?" he teased. As cute as it was, it was the truth. I had to get back to the flat and prepare for tomorrow's summit. "I do." I told him, and we walked back to the trolley station. It didn't take very long for the train to come. "I had fun." he said, hugging me goodbye, then he started for the station's exit. I boarded the train, but seconds later, I felt someone grab me from behind. "Wha-" I exclaimed, but before I could question it, Adam had spun me around and kissed me. "Goodnight, Anaís. " then the doors of the train closed. It took me a second to process what had just occurred. Did he really just kiss me? Did I kiss him back? Did I want to kiss him? I must have because my face held a silly grin the entire 45 minutes trip back to the flat. I went to bed thinking about Adam, maybe that was his plan all along...either way, I wasn't upset about it.

"Time to wake up, Anaís." I opened my eyes to my alarm going off and my summit partner speaking very loudly at 4 in the morning. "Ugh, no. Go away," I grumbled, but he ripped the blankets off me. "Hey, no one told you to scamper off with Aaaadam until the middle of the night. You hussie." he teased. Nick, my summit partner, was quite the character. He was 6'2", blonde and Dutch. He also didn't have to work today, so I wasn't sure why he was bothering me at 4 in the morning, but he was right. I had to get up and get moving. My conference started at 7 am, and I was the keynote speaker. I quickly got ready and zipped out the door. Today was a super important day, and I simply couldn't be late. I miraculously found my way to the correct bus. It actually took me three buses then I had to walk 8 blocks to find the O2 Ritz.

When I walked in, I set my things down and grabbed a tea. I realized I wasn't going to get through this day without tea and food, so I grabbed a bagel, and found my way to a little cozy corner backstage. I heard a voice from the shadows. "Hello, darling," the voice said, "you probably don't recognize me." The stage lights revealed what appeared to be a man, but when they stepped closer, I realized it was Katia. "My goodness, Goddess. You gave me such a fright. Darn near spooked the pantyhose off me!" I giggled. Goddess indeed. Katia was a tall, leggy woman from the Ukraine, with an hourglass figure that I could only dream about. She was dressed in workout clothes waiting for her dress to be steamed. Katia was also a transgender person-soon to be-Icon. A person I adored since the first moment we met. Katia had a complicated life and also a wife that she was very committed to. Katia had learned to unapologetically be herself. She was quite the force to be reckoned with.

As the summit was coming to an end for the day, I received a text from Adam. "Care for a stroll?" he asked, but I had something better in mind. "How about a dance?" I responded. I took a couple of the people from the summit with me back to the flat. I switched shoes then we set off for a night of adventure. Nick, of course, was all about it. We pub hopped for a few hours losing track of the number of drinks we had. When Helen, one of the interns, dropped to the floor, we all decided it was time to leave. The group stumbled its way through the dark corridors of "La Boulie", and everyone hopped into taxis. "Call me tomorrow." Adam requested pulling my hips towards him. Nick began to make kissing noises, and the group joined him. I could feel myself blushing, so I pecked him on the cheek and pushed Nick into the taxi. "I think you like him." Nick said teasingly. He wasn't far off. Adam was certainly growing on me.

When we got into the flat, I put my phone on the charger and took my blood sugar. I figured it would be high from the drinking. 172...whew. "Well, better than it being too low, I guess." I thought to myself. Nick walked in to help me hook myself up to my apnea monitor since I struggled to reach my backpack. "How is all this going for you, anyway?" he asked, gently placing the probes around my back. I don't know if it was the booze or the fact that he was the first person to ask me about my health (besides Annalise) all year, but I cracked like a coconut, and I began to finally cry. "Oh, hunnie. Did I hurt you?" he asked. "No," I told him, "I am just tired." "Oh well, let's get some rest. You know Adam will be trying to whisk you away tomorrow." In that instant, it was as if someone ripped open a dam. The tears were flowing, and I couldn't make them stop. "Oh sweetie. Here, sit down. What is it?" Nick asked, trying to wipe my tears away with a cloth.

I couldn't hold it in any longer. I needed to tell someone. I needed to make sense of what was happening. I told Nick of my health, of my history with my parents, and how my grand-père's widow found me. I told him about Demetri and Laurent. Then finally, I told him about HIM, and for the first time in 2 years, I allowed myself to say his name out loud - Gael. Nick sat back against the couch and let out a deep breath. "Anaís, I don't know where to begin. How are you keeping all this inside? I would have gone off on a bender or worse by now." he confessed. I dropped my head thinking back to the night I started coughing up blood. I knew something was wrong that night. I remember sitting on the bathroom floor with a hand full of pills. "It would be so simple." I told myself, "I would just go to sleep and not wake up. No more hospitals and no more pain."

It had been a full moon on a not-so-special Wednesday. I was staring up at the moon, asking God's universe where was my life headed? I couldn't hear my heart anymore. I felt so disconnected from life as if I weren't living at all, but merely existing. My phone light flickered, and there was Gael's name across the screen. "Are you okay?" was the first thing he said

195

when I answered. "I was about to ask you the same thing." I responded, ignoring his question. Neither of us was okay, but neither of us wanted to admit it. The ironic thing was, I was sitting under that moon telling myself that he was fine and not to call him, but here he was calling me.

"Does he know? At least about what's happening?" Nick asked. "No, We haven't spoken in months." I told him trying to not show my disappointment. "Do you think he should know? I understand that there is a hard past there, but wouldn't you want to know?" he asked, pushing my phone towards me. I thought about it for a moment then I picked up my phone. I wasn't sure how to have this conversation. What if he didn't respond. I was in Manchester, UK. He was in Concord, NH. I wasn't even sure what time it was in Concord. I closed my eyes and typed the message then hit send. "Why did we end?" I wrote. Seconds later, I started to go through the emotions. First panic "Why did you do that, Anaís? You shouldn't have messaged him!" An hour passed, then disappointment started. "See! You did this to yourself. Why would you open that do-"

My phone started lighting up"...." He was typing something. "Which time?" My heart started racing. "It's funny you write to me the day we were supposed to get married 4 years ago." I sat there starring blankly at the phone. Nick leaned over to see the screen. "He responded!" Nick exclaimed, "Girl respond to him! This is good." But was it? We had done this a million times over. "Text!!" Nick pushed. "Okay, Okay!" I said, taking a deep breath and sitting up. Here goes...

"Really?" I started, "Wow, that's crazy. Well...why did we?" I asked, feeling half surprised and half not. The timing was always strange with us.

196

"We ended off hurt and ego. Hurt people, hurt people." Gael explained. I understood that phrase all too well. I looked around the room for an excuse to get off the phone. Nick grabbed my hand and whispered, "It's okay. You can do this." He started texting again. *"I found myself when we were together, I didn't know who I was. I didn't beat the drum that you told me to hit. When we were together, things weren't stable. Now look at you, your career has taken off. Can you not say you found yourself, either?"*

"That's not my question, dear." I didn't want him to make the conversation about me. There were things I needed to know before I told him what was going on. Not to mention, I had always known who I wanted to be...just not how to reach her. So honestly,...no. I hadn't found myself, per se. I left last year to do just that, and while sure the process had certainly started, I didn't think I was quite there...yet.

"There aren't enough words to even begin to answer...dear." He was doing it. He was being sarcastic to deflect.

"Why?" I asked. I was preparing myself for the end of the conversation to happen next, but it didn't. Instead, he said, *"Ugh, I'm pouring myself a whiskey."*

"Pour me one." I typed, trying to be cool even though I was anxious for an answer.

"Neat or on the rocks?" he jokingly asked.

"Neat, please," I responded, aiming to put the conversation back on target *"with a slice of truth."* 8 minutes had passed, just when I was about to put my phone down, the screen lit up. He actually responded with a real response this time.

"Too many feelings and emotions that haven't left. I didn't even know who I was inside yet, but instead of celebrating when you lost your memory, I came to meet you the next day. I lost my best friend, my lover, and even side piece through all the bullshit, and was left with nothing to say because you don't remember any of it except the small pieces left in emails. Years down the road and times have changed, but the full moon is still there."

I knew that reference. He'd told me before that when we first met, when he first told me he loved me, when we first got together, and when he first proposed, all happened randomly, but all under full moons. It had become "our thing". My mind flashed back briefly to the conversation he and I had almost a year ago; it too, was under a full moon. I cleared my mind of the memory. I had very specific questions I needed answered.

"Okay. Two questions. Did you hate me for forgetting, and do you think it was best, our breakup, overall?" I was pushing. I knew it was risky. Gael was every bit as much of a runner as I was, if not more...but I needed answers.

"No. But this isn't a one-way interview." he said pushing back. "No, he said no." I thought to myself. "What's happening?" Nick asked. He was in the kitchen, making tea and food. Normally, I would have joined him, but not this time. I couldn't eat. I had to focus, or I'd lose my nerve.

"Be cool. Be calm." I told myself as I typed my next words. *"It's quite interesting that you say that...I'll tell you why after you answer my question. You can WhatsApp me if its easier."* He agreed that being verbal would be a lot easier. I gave him my number and instructions on how to use the app. Then, I waited. I reached over the couch and grabbed my charger. Things were going pretty well, so far, and I did not want that ruined by my phone dying. 23 minutes passed, but finally, he was video calling. I took a deep breath. "Okay girl, it's going to be fine." I told myself, then I answered the call.

"There she is." he said with a smile on his face. His eyes were still as blue/green as ever. They did this thing where they would change colors with his mood. It had been a while since we spoke, let alone saw each other. The last time, we had an unexpected "Sleepover". My mind escaped me. I began to recall our last physical night together. I had been frustrated with him and his lack of actions. He promised one of our elder friends that he would take him to the movies, but he flaked without even giving Mr. Kingsly a call. It was one thing to not keep your word to me, but it was another to disappoint an elder. I'd been so angry that I sent him a long text, swearing him off. By the time I was done, I felt foolish. I went through these spurts of aggression with him sometimes. I credit it to me not understanding how or why he was able to get under my skin the way he did. It shouldn't have been a surprise that he didn't keep his word. After all, that was Gael's signature move. Come to think of it, he'd always been that way, so why did I expect anything different?

I spoke to a friend about my frustrations. "Sex!" he exclaimed. "What the hell?" I asked, feeling annoyed. "What does sex have to do with anything?" "You two keep fighting. One minute he's mad at you and the next you are mad at him. It's because ya'll haven't had sex. Think about it. He remembers, and you don't. He's frustrated because he's used to being with you in a certain way and now he can't." I laughed, "Well if that is his problem, what is mine?" I asked, walking straight into a trap. "You just need sex period." he said, laughing. I ended the call with Spencer. Was he correct? Could all of this be simply because of sexual frustration? I mean, it's not like I didn't find Gael attractive and I had been almost basically his wife….I opened my closet. "No, you can't do this…can you?" I spoke aloud to myself. I decided I would text Gael, and depending on how he responded, I would base my actions off that.

"Come over." I wrote.

"What? You just told me to go to hell, and now you want me to come over??" he responded.

Realizing how crazy he must have thought I was, I told him that we needed to talk, and that I hated fighting with him. He told me that he was getting things ready for work, but that I could come over. I found myself smiling. "Stop it!" I ordered myself, "What is wrong with you? You can't do this." But I wanted to. I opened my closet doors, staring at my clothes. If I was going to do this, I had to dress the part, but how? I spotted a pair of silver heels, a red dress, and my black trench coat. "What the hell…" I said to myself, grabbing them all. Thirty minutes later, I was out the door and heading to Gael's.

When I arrived, he opened to door to greet me. He ran back into the kitchen; I could smell the dryer on and the stove. I wandered down the hall and into the kitchen where he was standing, wrapped in only a towel. I tried not to look. "You got this. Stop being weird." I told myself as Gael escorted me to the living room. He went to let his dog, Rufus, outside. I found myself examining him with my eyes. Was he always so cut and muscular? I was so preoccupied, that I hadn't even considered the fact that he could have planned his wardrobe...or lack thereof...just as I did. I tried to catch myself before he caught me looking. He turned and smiled, walking to the other couch and sitting.

"So, you look nice." he said, pointing at my heels, "Special occasion?" "Yes," I said shortly, "I am going to Mardi Gras tonight." which was partially true. I had grabbed my bag on the way out the door, figuring I would use up some miles and go to New Orleans when I left his house. I smiled internally at the disappointment apparent on his face.

"Fun. So, what do you want to talk about?" he asked. I straightened up and dove into it. "Look. I don't like it when we fight like that. We fight because I lose my temper. I lose my temper because you don't keep communication or your word. Gael, that's not cool. If we are going to be friends, then we need to be real friends. That means respecting each other above all things. I don't like being made to feel like I am a thing of convenience. Okay?" "You're right, and I apologize. I will work on it." he said, seemingly sincere.

"Wow, that was easy." I thought. I stood up to leave, "Well, I am going to get out of here and try to make the flight." We leaned over to give each other a hug, but it became awkward, and we chose to stand up to hug. I loved the feeling of his arms around me. I took a step closer and melted into them as he squeezed tighter. Honestly, I should have seen it coming. He was in a towel when I arrived for heaven's sake. "You don't think your dress is a little short? Your coat is longer than it." he said reaching for my butt, "Wait a minute..." "BINGO!" I thought as he grabbed at me, "Focus, you got this girl. Be sexy!" I told myself. I took a few steps back and said in a low sexy voice, "Well now you have to find the rest."

Gael, unbuttoned my coat revealing the dress he thought I had on was left at home on my bed and all that was under the coat was my royal blue lingerie. "Oh, wow." he said softly pulling me in for a kiss. Things got passionate quickly. He removed my coat and begun to kiss my neck. Each kiss resulted in a purr which led to him biting and me clawing his back. He leaned me forward, our eyes locking. His eyes a cold blue, his hands tightly gripping my waist. "We have to stop..." he said, "Everything in me wants to take you upstairs and lay you across my bed." but it was too late to stop. The flame had been ignited, fire flowing like blood throughout my body. Whether or not I was willing to admit it, Spencer was right. I wanted Gael as much as he wanted me. I whispered into Gael's ear, "What's stopping you?" clawing his back with one hand and removing his towel with the other. On cue, he lifted me into the air, wrapping my legs around his waist and carried me to his bedroom.

Hours later, I woke up and looked around, I was still in Gael's arms. I couldn't believe what I'd just done. I most certainly wasn't going to make the flight. I felt like a goddess. He rolled over, kissed me, then went back to sleep. I climbed on top of him and nibbled on his chest. "Wake up." I urged him, kissing his neck. "No, I have to get up for work in a bit." he said curtly. His tone shocked me. I slid off him, and he rolled in the other direction. Did I do something wrong? This was unusual for us. It was usually me trying to sleep and him sneaking under the blankets. I felt a knot in my chest. I needed to leave, all of a sudden I didn't feel sexy anymore. He had tried so many times to get me to open up sexually and when I finally did...he shot me down. I felt disgusting. I felt rejected. I felt like I did something terrible. I needed to get out of there. I felt so ashamed of myself.

I slid off his bed and began quietly grabbing my things. The longer it took, the worse I felt. My head started pounding as if someone was beating it with a bat. My vision started to blur, but I didn't care; I just wanted to get to my car and forget about this night. I didn't bother putting my lingerie back on, I just stuffed everything in my pocket, and carried my shoes down the stairs as quietly as possible. Why did all this feel so familiar? Why was my head hurting so badly? I got to the hallway and looked out the window on the door. It was freezing and iced over. "Fuck." I thought as I slipped on my heels. When I stood up to open the door, I heard Gael coming down the stairs quickly.

"What the hell are you doing?" he asked, pulling my body away from the door. I didn't like when he got aggressive. He'd put his hands on me before and not in a good way. My guard flew up, and I felt myself entering defense mode. "I'm leaving." I said, refusing to meet his eyes. "No, stop it." he argued, "Look at me." He turned me to face him. Staring me in the eyes, he asked with a forceful tone, "What's going on? What's wrong?" I snatched away from him, "Nothing. I'm fine. I just want to leave." I was starting to feel even more uncomfortable and extremely aware of how naked I was under my coat. "Baby, come on. Tell me what's wrong." he urged. He always had a way of getting me to talk. "I feel bad. I want to go home. I feel dirty like I did something wrong." "Because we had sex?" he said slightly laughing, "Don't be silly."

He looked at my face and could tell that I wasn't amused. My body language had become distant and cold. He wasn't getting it. It was more than that. It was how he responded. I was waiting until marriage when he and I got together, and

I decided to sleep with him. I knew early on that I had the runner gene when people got too close. I had been hurt before. This made sex quite difficult for me. "Okay, I'm sorry for whatever I did." he said, but I was still set on going home. The damage was done. I needed to get home into some clothes and into my own bed.

He pulled me into him. He was still naked, but the desire to claw him wasn't there. "Listen to me. I love you." He lifted my chin so our lips could meet. "Call me later on." he said as I walked out the door. I looked back and tried to smile at him. He didn't know it, but this was goodbye. I lifted my foot to take a step, but I slipped and rolled down the stairs. I already felt shameful, and now, I was mortified. "Oh shit!" he yelled. He was still completely naked, and there were several people and children outside getting ready for their day. As he ran to get shorts, I tried lifting myself up to get into my car. The pain was excruciating. I looked down at my legs and saw that I had a few cuts. When Gael returned, he picked me up and took me back inside to the couch. "Damn it baby, are you okay?" he asked. We realized that I rolled my ankle and had some scrapes, but besides that, I'd survive...at least physically.

Embarrassed was putting it lightly. "I need to call Derek," I said. I was still set on getting out of there. "Yea? You want him to pick you up dressed like that?" he joked. I looked down and realized that it would have been pretty difficult to explain to the guy who saw me as a little sister (at the time) why I was wearing nothing but a trench coat. I started feeling down. "This is what I get for trying to be sexy." I said grumpily. "Baby you are sexy, you just had a spill." he said, still laughing. I shot him an evil look, and before I could stop myself, the words flew out of my mouth. "Then why did you reject me this morning?"

I blurted out. "Is that what you were upset about? Anaís, I told you I had to go to work today" he replied. Looking at the clock on the wall, "Not that I will make it."

I felt guilty. Now, I even more wanted to go home. "You don't have to deal with me. I can call a taxi and have Derek get my car later." I told him. I grabbed my coat and shoes, then tried to stand up. "Whoa now. Stop it. You're not going anywhere. Sit still." he ordered, "First of all, you can't walk, nor do you have any pants to put on." He walked into the kitchen and returned with a pill for the pain and a glass of water. "You are staying here, and we are going back to sleep. I will take you home in a few hours." As much as I didn't like it, he had a point, and it's not like I could get Derek on the phone that early anyway. I tucked my pride, and allowed him to wrap my ankle, then carry me back to his bed. This time he wrapped me in his arms, and we slept. Gael was the only person I slept with and outside of one other relationship that I couldn't remember, he remained. After that night, the *only* person I slept with.

Gael could be a jackass, but he was also protective. It was hard to comprehend how the person who once saved my life from a car hitting me, had years later turned into the person whose fists I needed to fear the most.

"Was any of it real?" I asked. Trying to push the other thoughts from my mind. My head was starting to hurt, but I wasn't going to allow it to get in the way of this talk. It was too important.

"Of course it was." he said firmly, *"I don't know why you think it wasn't?"*

"Because it doesn't make sense why we didn't last. " I blurted

loudly enough to startle Nick. "Sorry." I mouthed to him. *"We were either in love, or we weren't."* I informed Gael.

"I told you, I did love you and I still do. Its.... it's complicated." he said distantly. I could tell there was more to the story. Truth be told I already knew what he was hiding.

"Our relationship wasn't normal," he continued, *"we had a connection that bonded us at the soul. Why do you think we always come back to here, no matter how long it's been or how things ended. That's real love, that's us!"*

I heard what he was saying, and he was correct. We were bonded at the soul, so much that we always knew when something was up with the other person even though there was no proof on our personal ends. It's precisely why he called me the night I had the pills in my hand even though there was no way for him to truly know something was wrong. It's also how I knew what was going on with him without us ever having spoken about it. I knew I was pushing a dangerous line, but we'd come too far already. I needed him to say the words. I needed him to confirm or deny what I already knew. I couldn't tell him what was going on with me until I heard the words from his own mouth, so I pushed even harder.

"Well, it doesn't sound that complicated to me. I do appreciate you having this conversation, but you've not really explained how it's complicated, so all I can do is believe that the love was just a fantasy." I said only half believing the words I was saying. Of course, it was real, at least from my end.

"It was real." he continued, *"It is real. It's just complicated!"* I heard him, but I wasn't willing to continue to accept "complicated" as an answer.

"How?" I argued back, *"Why is it so complicated."* Realizing we were going in circles, I went there. *"Gael, listen I already*

know. Just tell me, please."

"*Fuck!*" he yelled, *"I got married!"*

And there it was. It felt like a thousand knives had entered my heart simultaneously. I froze and dropped the phone. I knew it, I knew it all along. I don't know how, but I just knew. I told Amanda, the friend I was staying with back in November/December, that I could feel in my core that something was wrong and changing with him. I told her I thought he was getting married, but I couldn't explain to her that I didn't have any proof...just a feeling. I even told his best friend who I had slightly, oddly enough, become buddies with. Cora had me listening to songs, but I would never ask her outright questions about Gael. My only request was that she looked out for him. Cora and I spent most of Gael's and my relationship hating each other. It wasn't until recently that she apologized and we came to terms. She even went as far as saying, "I have never met two people that belong together more than you and Gael. I believe you will find your ways." Which was huge coming from the person who was convinced that I was trying to steal her best friend away from her.

I hadn't realized that I hadn't taken a breath for several moments. Nick shook me, and when I finally drew breath, all I could exhale were mountains of tears and sorrow. I was crushed. "Hello?"Gael called. Nick rushed to wipe my face with my blanket and shoved the phone in my hands, urging me to continue to talk to Gael. "Yes, I am here." I managed to get out. "I am sorry I didn't mean to make you drop the phone." he said. "It's fine. You have nothing to apologize for. You did nothing wrong. I already knew, Gael." I tried to sound strong, but I was barely holding on. "I know you did. You always know. I still can't believe I had to get married to get the papers I needed." he confessed. "I don't understand." I told him. I couldn't tell if he was being truthful or not. "Anaís, it's not what you think. It's just papers."

He tried explaining, but even though I heard his words, I wasn't feeling anything except extreme sorrow. "Hold on a second," I lied, "I need to grab my teacup." I didn't have a teacup, I just needed to put the phone down. I leaned forward into my pillow, and I let out a deep sob. I hadn't cried this much since my sister died. I was in physical agony, and what I would later come to learn - I was grieving. It felt as if everything, every memory was attacking me at once. My head was killing me. Memories flashed through my mind at a rapid speed. I was drowning, and I couldn't find anything to grab on to.

Nick rushed over to me. "My darling, you have to tell him now." he encouraged. "I -i- can't." I was struggling to form words. "Do you want me to?" he asked, but I couldn't let him do it. Gael could not hear that I was dying and about to get an extremely risky surgery that would almost insure my demise. "He can't know." I repeated. "Okay, hunnie." Nick said, holding my hands. He put me sitting upwards and handed me the phone. Gael and I sat in silence for a while. When I finally spoke, I told him that I didn't know what to say, neither did he. The silence continued. It continued for another 15 minutes or so. I tried to speak, but the words escaped me. It was as if someone poured acid down my throat. Gael spoke first, "You know I love you, right?" I wanted to believe him. I wanted so badly to go back and not know what I now knew, but that's not how life works. "Everything's different now." I muttered...and it was, nothing would ever be the same. I felt myself fall into the beginnings of a numbing state. "I have to go." I told him. It was physically killing me to be on the phone. Besides, what else could there be to say? He was marrying, if not already had, someone else. Things could never be the way they were before. "I don't want this to be the end." he said sorrowfully. "Please, let me call you tomorrow. Anaís, I love you." he begged. The words stung like a million jellyfish latching on one after the other. I couldn't think, I was barely breathing; trying to do everything to hold back the tears. Much to my dismay, no matter what happens to me, this was in fact, the end of Gael and Anaís. I looked at the screen through tear-soaked eyes and uttered my final words, *"I love you. Goodbye."* pressing the end button on us physically and literally.

Nick grabbed the phone, and I collapsed into my pillow, letting out a deep painful cry. I laid there like that for three hours straight...just crying. When I finally stopped, I went completely numb. There were moments where I wasn't even sure I was breathing. Nick would roll me on my side and try to get me to drink water, but I couldn't. I couldn't move my body, not even to make it to the summit. This lasted for 48 hours before Nick called Adam telling him what happened. Adam was determined to help, but I was beyond repair. He had instructed Nick to bring me over to his house and that we were going to spend the night there. Reluctantly, I obliged. I knew I needed to physically move my body, but I lacked the will. When we arrived at Adam's, he wanted to surprise me with his version of spaghetti. I realized that I was being destructive, and it was unfair to Adam, who had only been kind. I tried to box my feelings away and be apart of supper. Soon after we all piled into Adam's bed. Adam tried to wrap his arms around me, but it was the very last thing I wanted. I laid there, wide awake feeling utterly empty. Something had changed. If this was a vampire series, at this pivotal moment, my humanity was turning off. When the sun came up, I grabbed my case and headed straight for Paris.

A week later, I ended up in the emergency room. Things were officially at its peak. I contacted those closest to me. I attempted to write two letters - one for my brother, and the second I simply stared at. This letter was for Gael, but what was I going to say to him? I put the piece of paper back in my folder, and I laid back. Dr. Horowitz entered the room, "Are you ready?" he asked. I turned my head to look out the window. The sun was starting to rise, I thought for a second, "This could be it." but I decided that I had come too far to turn back now. "Yes, Doctor. I am ready."

31

And now...

Three weeks had passed since the surgery. "How are we doing?" nurse Olga asked. I sat up as she opened my blinds, trying to remember what it was like to be outside. "I could use some BBQ." I joked. Nurse Olga didn't find my jokes amusing, but today she smiled. "How about beignets?" she retorted, handing me papers. "What are these?" I thought. Across the top, it read Discharge Instructions. "I get to leave?" I looked out the window then leaned back on the bed. Was I ready for this? Sure it had been three weeks of being locked inside with hospital food. Three weeks of Nurse Olga catching me trying to get to the lifts only to send me back to my room. Three weeks of no contact with the outside world except Annalise, but it had also been three weeks of not thinking of what I was going to do next. "Yes, but if you want to stay here with me, I can arrange for more borscht to be brought to you." Borscht was the absolute last thing I wanted. I hated beets and wasn't a fan of soup.

Nurse Olga was a stickler for healthy eating and did not appreciate me trying to hack the vending machines down the hall. She entered my room two weeks after my surgery with a to-go container. I excitedly opened the tub to reveal a red, cold soup-like dish. "Go on, eat. You need your strength." she instructed. I found the taste to be revolting. Over the next few days, I tried to be creative and hide the stew until I could flush it. One night I'd lost my balance, almost falling. I grabbed onto the shelf, knocking over everything. Nurse Olga entered into the room. "You vomit?" she asked. I couldn't stand the pressure when she looked directly at me.

Yana Olga stood at 5'8" and was 200 lbs easily. The woman was built like a linebacker, enjoying shot put as a hobby. She was a kind woman, but absolutely terrifying. "No, I'm just not hungry." I said. "No! You eat, or you get tube. You eat, and sadness will go away. EAT!" she ordered. She left the room and returned with more soup, standing there until I ate every bit.

"No, that's okay!" I said, standing up to pack my things. It was time to leave the hospital. I said "goodbye" to my doctors and nurses, thanking them for all of their patience and help. "Where are you headed?" one of the nurses asked. "Eh, wherever the wind takes me." I responded, but I knew exactly where I was going - the Eiffel Tower.

I got out of the car, walked across the greenery, and took a long inhale. Outside of the fumes from the traffic, the air felt great. Over the next few days, I took as many walks as possible. I reached out to my spiritual adviser and a few friends to let them know I was out. "When are you returning?" they'd often ask, but I would always say "soon". The truth is I wasn't sure when I was returning…if I ever was. I laid on the grass, looking up at the sky and the Eiffel Tower. "I really could just stay here forever." I thought to myself. My surroundings were so peaceful. It was a beautiful day, perfect for doing absolutely nothing...so that's exactly what I did.

Another two weeks had gone by, and I was still no closer to considering returning to the States. I sat in the living room, listening to the rain outside the window. "What are you going to do today?" Annalise asked, "It looks like you might be stuck indoors. Perhaps a good time for writing?" She had a point. I went into my grand-père's study and looked for my folder with my notebooks. I sat down in his chair, remembering when Annalise first brought me here.

The house was an older cottage just on the tip of Paris. It had been built in the 1700's. My great-grandparents procured the property in the late '50s, passing it on to my grand-père upon their death. It was a charming home with a good amount of natural light. It was primarily made of stone then later updated. Once inside, the entrance hall led through to a double living room with fireplace, a closed kitchen opening onto a terrace, a separate toilet, and a dressing room. On the first floor, a landing led to two bedrooms, a bathroom, two shower rooms, and a separate toilet. Up another level to the second floor, a landing gave access to two bedrooms and a shared bathroom. On the garden level, a corridor led to a large family room, my grand-père's study, and the tea room via sliding windows onto the gardens with their lawns and trees and plants. Around the back of the house, you could find an underground cellar where the family's wine was kept. Past the cellar, you would see my grand-père's workshop and the barn. A little past that revealed a beautiful lake where he built a hammock so Annalise could read her novels.

My grand-père had kept the property up after his father died from pneumonia. So much history was in this place. I often liked to picture what it would have been like to grow up here. I'd barge into his study, climbing in his lap with melons dripping from my hands. "Well, aren't we a sticky one?" he'd say, lifting me into the air then carrying me into the kitchen to clean my hands and face. I'd ride on his shoulders to his workshop, where he'd sit me on top of the counter so I could watch him work until Annalise rang the dinner bell. I would race him to the house where Annalise would greet us at the door. "Oh! We must clean up first, darlings." she'd sing pointing to the wood shavings all over my grand-père and I. "Oui, madame." we'd say slipping past her, but not before grand-père would sneak a fresh dinner roll. Of course, she'd catch us. Annalise would always know when we were being mischievous, but grand-père would spin and dance with her making her giggle. He'd whisper, "You are my light." and kiss her upon her forehead. After supper, they would tuck me in while Annalise sang me to sleep. It was a lovely fantasy.

"Daydreaming are we?" Annalise called, startling me. I smiled. "I don't remember where I put my binder with my notebook?" I said, searching under the desk. "Oh, I put them in the drawer." She said, opening one of grand-père's desk drawers. "You know, he used to daydream too. He was always imagining a new creation, whether it was a piece of art or a new flavor of wine. Your grand-père was always dreaming. I wish you could have met him. He would be so proud of the woman you are and are becoming." She kissed the top of my head and went into the kitchen to make evening tea.

I pulled out my notebooks, and a piece of paper fell out. I hadn't recognized the parchment type. It must have been something old and left in the drawer, which wouldn't have been a surprise since Annalise left much of my grand-père's things exactly as he last had them. A good bit had been donated, but still so much remained as if he were going to walk through those doors at any moment. "What must it be like to have that kind of love?" I thought as I opened the piece of paper.

"Laissez la lune guider votre esprit, mais n'ayez pas peur des ténèbres, les étoiles sont là pour vous guider" – R.B. 1964

I smiled at the RB, realizing that it stood for René Borde. I pulled out my books and opened my folder to the blank page reading only: "Dear Gael." I still didn't know what to say to him. As hurt as I was, there was still a big part of me that cared. I knew it was unhealthy, and I needed to move on with my life. But still, there were tender parts that I wasn't quite ready to face.

It rained for three days straight. I took this time to bond with Annalise, learning how to make the most delicious dishes. We talked about my grand-père and how they met. I laughed when she told me of how he fell through the barn roof and refused to allow anyone to tend to him until she was present. We talked of his heartbreak when he came back from the States and how it was that what led him to paint. We talked about my parents and some of the things that happened to me and my siblings. We even danced around the living room to swing music, laughing and playing in my great grand-père suits. It was a marvelous time.

Noticing that my mind was preoccupied, Annalise sat a tray of pastries and tea down next to me. "A treat for your thought." she said, offering me mini prosciutto-wrapped melons. I was staring at the blank pieces of paper I laid out before me. One was addressed to Gael, and the others were titled, "What next." I had avoided the topic for so long, but I knew it was time to officially close that door and get on with my life. The trouble is, I didn't know what I wanted to do next. "You will know when it is time. Maybe just start writing, and it will come to you. I've found that La Sein is a great place to relax." she said. I grabbed my books and snacks, then headed for the city.

She was right, it was very peaceful. I looked around at the city lights and the others walking the streets, then back down to my paper. "What do you want to do with your life?" I asked myself aloud. "If you could do anything, anything at all…what would it be?"

I began listing my desires:

1) Go back to school
2) Build a program that would feed the world
3) Buy/Build a Chateau
4) Move to Paris
5) Find closure and peace

"Closure and Peace…" I whispered to myself.

Days prior, Gael had reached out to me asking how I was doing. I didn't respond to him at first, but when I did, I purged all that I had been feeling. I told him that things needed to be different, and he could no longer continue to randomly contact me. I explained that it felt like someone was ripping open a wound every time he tried, and I needed to be able to get on with my life. I told him what was going on with my health and how I had survived surgery with the odds that were 60% against me. Of course, a part of me was still in love with him, but I was working my way through that, and in order to do so, I had to give myself closure. He told me he wanted to be in my life and to see me.

His words reminded me of that night I decided to leave for the first time and our phone call. It's funny how we always know, and it's always revealed under the sky of a full moon.

When we hung up the phone, I felt so hurt. He hadn't said anything wrong, but I knew everything was changing. He ended the conversation telling me, "You have to come back. You have missions to complete." But how? How was I going to complete anything when just hours prior, I was contemplating ending it all? I was also angry at him. I wanted to yell at him. I wanted to tell him, "NO! You don't get to tell me to make sure I come back! You don't get to call me like this, leaving me always confused about us." He told me he didn't want to be just a friend, but he also could not be a stranger. What else could there be considering he wasn't taking action to be anything more than a friend. We'd promised to meet up several times in Phoenix, but he always stood me up. Why ask to meet me if you aren't even going to show up? I would, a year later, find out that he was marrying and it would change everything.

I also thought about Laurent. I hadn't told him that I was back in town. We had a great time together, but I was sure he'd ask why I said "no" that night, and it would have been too difficult to explain to him. If I was being honest with myself...I was always torn. I wanted the affection because, like darkness, the desire consumes me. I reveled within the immediate gratification of my actions, but later...I hated myself. My core conscious knows what I want, but my darkness struggles to wait. She emerges, provocatively tainting everything she touches and when she's had her fill...when the sun comes up...all I am left with is regret. It is almost drug-like, and the crash is horrible.

Perhaps...though that's my life story. I struggle to balance the light and dark...so I choose the light. I suppress all desires that would release my darkness, and I wait. Gael would tell me that my actions never made sense. If I wanted him that I should just be with him because we would be getting married soon. But that's the issue. When was soon? We'd gone back and forth so many times that I stopped believing it would happen. I felt like a yo-yo that he would pick up whenever he was bored…and I was tired of it.

The reality is, it wasn't his fault. I felt so hurt and empty. The responsibility was all mine. I had spent my life pouring into others and allowing them to take more than what I could give. I allowed others to break my heart. I told them it was okay by accepting those behaviors. I did this, and only I could change it. I spent the next hour drafting letters HER- the lost me.

My darling heart,

I have loved like I should, but lived like I shouldn't. I have not always put you first and caused your destruction. From the bottom of my soul, I am sorry. I vow to spend the rest of my life, finding true love and joy. I have been given another chance at life, and I promise to not waste a moment of it. I forgive myself for things I cannot control, and with this life, I give you my promise; I promise to always be cautious, but never afraid. I promise to love unapologetically.

I promise to only put you in the hands of someone who will undoubtedly care for you. I promise to stop looking back. I promise to embrace all that I am. I promise to stop surviving and start living. I promise to always dance and follow the moon.

Love,

Anais

I burned the letter and blew its remains into the air. "Is it time?" Annalise asked, standing behind me. She grabbed my hand and turned to watch the Eiffel Tower touch all of Paris with its dazzling lights. "You are leaving, aren't you?"

218

she whispered. I turned to face her. "It's okay darling, I understand. Anaís, I would love nothing more than to keep you here with me, but you are your grand-père's legacy, and if you are anything like him, I have no doubt that you will end up right where you are supposed to be." Our eyes filled with tears as we hugged one another.

I thought of the hurt, and all I put myself through. That's how it started. Felt like I was merely existing and floating through this world. The days seemed to pass rapidly, and I felt no closer to where I needed to be. I was drowning in a sea of sorrow...so I left. I had to go find the spark that would ignite my fire. I felt such peace in Paris, but if I was honest with myself, it was a hole for me to stick my head in. Little things I found to satisfy my cravings for life...but nothing could make me full. I traveled the world to realize that the problem was staring me back in the mirror. I wasn't happy with myself. It wasn't 100% Santa Monica, but Anaís...and I needed to find her. I needed to find the Paradise I'd dreamed of, but within myself. Traveling helped drown out the noise so I could clear my head. I knew what I had to do...and I knew it wouldn't be that easy. It's taken a lot of reflection, but I had finally made it. Thinking about this entire journey, I am now a lot more comfortable with who I am...knowing that I should practice not control, so much as balance, and be unapologetically true to my heart.

We continued to watch the shimmering lights of the tower. There was a shift in the wind. You know that moment when it all just clicks. Literally, you're standing there, and you feel this wave of power come over you. You feel the guilt, the sorrow, and the anguish fade away as the power of your success, happiness, and love take its place. There's mild adrenaline surging through your body, and you can't help but smile. Your hand and toes are tingling with delight. You sniff the air, and it somehow smells sweeter. You look around, and you're no longer worried. Yea..that's what it felt like - something's happening, I can feel it. Whatever it is...I'm ready. Things were changing for sure, but that's life, a constant change. For the first time, I knew exactly what I wanted and how to reach it. I looked up at the full moon and smiled knowing that no matter where I went, all would be fine because I found her at last - my Paradise - and I was never letting her go again. I was finally at peace.

To my darlings

My darlings,

First, I want to thank you for joining me on this journey. I hope I was able to inspire you to go forward with your life, embracing all that you are…unapollogetically.

There are going to be days, weeks and, sometimes, even months that it feels as if the entire universe has cast you aside. During these moments, I want you to remember that you are not alone. Growth happens when we are most uncomfortable. There are going to be people that attempt to put you into a box, but do not let them! You are more than what the outside world perceives. #ICanBeBoth

Each and every one of you has a purpose for your existence. It won't always appear so clear, but just remember that you matter. This world would not be the same without you. No matter what demon you are battling, you have to keep fighting. Your strength and courage is the light that keeps this world positive.

It is my hope that you will start your own journey, finding your Paradise. Remember,

"You can sit in the corner and cry, or you can go out and dance in the raid. Either way, the storm is coming." -P.R 2008

I have faith in you all.

Much love,
    Paradise Rodriguez

If you are experiencing suicidal thoughts, remember that you are not broken...just in pain. Allow yourself to seek love and help.

www.TheCatchAFallingStarFoundation.com

If you or anyone you know is a victim of trafficking or domestic violence, SEEK HELP right away. You are not alone!

www.TheCatchAFallingStarFoundation.com

About the Author

Paradise E Rodriguez-Bordeaux (born August 17, 1996) is a French-American (born) fashion model, actress, activist, keynote speaker, and author. Her work can usually be found online and within luxury magazines throughout America, Europe, and New Zealand. She has walked for various fashion designers, including Jeff Garner and Quynh Paris. She is perhaps best known for her activism work with displaced children. Rodriguez-Bordeaux takes her inspiration from her early childhood and a more iconic role models like, "Creole Goddess," Josephine Baker, who worked with what was in front of them, refusing to give up on their passions and sought out to make a positive mark on the world. Paradise's work has a sophistication that sets them apart from a typical performer's lifestyle. With Paradise Rodriguez. Inc and Catch A Falling Star, Paradise combines a determined, forceful aesthetic with a humble philosophy, never compromising her ethical principles or her style credentials. She was born in the States but did not live a traditional childhood. Growing up without parents, she eventually began her search for her family in France, Spain, Puerto Rico, and Ireland. She eventually connected with relatives and is living between Paris and Manhattan, NYC. In 2014, Paradise suffered from a traumatic brain injury causing her to lose (5) five years of memories. While the memories never returned, she has been doing well in her fight against Ovarian Cancer. She then, she has won various awards for her outreach work including the 2018 Woman of Strength award and has since released her debut her book, "Finding Paradise."

You can connect with me on:

- https://www.paradiserodriguez.com
- https://twitter.com/home?lang=en
- https://www.facebook.com/paradiserodriguez1
- https://www.linkedin.com/in/paradiserodriguez
- https://www.instagram.com/paradise_rodriguez

Made in the USA
Middletown, DE
01 August 2020

14172107R00129